ROMANTIC GHOST STORIES

Julie Burtinshaw

GHOST HOUSE

Ghost House Books

The Publisher: Ghost House Books
Distributed by Lone Pine Publishing
10145 – 81 Avenue   1808 – B Street NW, Suite 140
Edmonton, AB Canada T6E 1W9   Auburn, WA USA 98001

Website: http://www.ghostbooks.net

National Library of Canada Cataloguing in Publication
Burtinshaw, Julie, 1958-
  Romantic ghost stories / Julie Burtinshaw.
  ISBN 1-894877-28-4

  1. Ghosts. 2. Legends. I. Title.
GR580.B87 2003   398.25   C2003-910685-3

Editorial Director: Nancy Foulds
Project Editor: Christopher Wangler
Illustrations Coordinator: Carol Woo
Production Manager: Gene Longson
Layout & Production: Chia-Jung Chang
Cover Design: Gerry Dotto

Photo Credits: The photographs and illustrations in this book are reproduced with the kind permission of the following sources: Library of Congress (p. 20: USZ62-78703; p. 54, 69: USZ6-1261; p. 78: USZ62-98917; p. 90, 103: DIG-ppmsc-07403; p. 146: USZ62-115614; p. 4-5, 177: HABS,NY,31-NEYO,51-1; p. 179: HABS,NY,31-NEYO,51-3; p. 181: USZ62-102555; p. 200: HABS, DC,WASH,613-4; p. 203: USZ62-124268; p. 197, 210: DIG-ppmsc-08275); Istock (p. 25: Sarah Skiba; p. 88: Sandra O'Claire; p. 100: Lise Gagnon; p. 131: Luigi Scuderi; p. 193: Nicola Brown); Oakland Convention and Visitors Bureau/Dunsmuir Historic Estate (p. 31); Anthony Barrett (p. 36); Silver Springs (p. 9, 47); Klondike Gold Rush National Historical Park (p. 52: David H. Curl); Dennis Bathory-Kitsz (p. 81, 84); Cincinatti Historical Society (p. 109); Delta Queen Steamboat Company (p. 110); Salem Public Library (p. 122: 8794); Washington State Parks and Recreation Commission (p. 138, 140, 148); Bibliothéque Nationale de Québec (p. 161); U.S. Fish and Wildlife Service (p. 168, 173: George Gentry); www.thecumbriadirectory.com (p. 224).

The stories, folklore and legends in this book are based on the author's research of sources including individuals whose experiences have led them to believe they have encountered phenomena of some kind or another. They are meant to entertain, and neither the publisher nor the authors claim these stories represent fact.

We acknowledge the financial support of the Government of Canada through the Book Publishing Industry Development Program (BPIDP) for our publishing activities.

PC:P5

To San Remo's
Valhalla of Kristari "Jet"
1992–2003
RIP

Contents

Chapter 4: Lovelorn

Chapter 5: A Romantic Miscellany

Chapter 6: Three's a Crowd

Acknowledgments

I would like to extend an enormous thank you to my friend Rod McFarland, without whom this book would never have been completed. His honesty, his sense of humor and his awesome command of the English language as he read through each of these stories proved invaluable. So for all that you did for me, including the tech support, "Thanks dude!"

I'd also like to acknowledge the staff of Ghost House Books and in particular Chris Wangler, my in-house editor. Chris always had time to talk to me (even on his days off), and he provided me with excellent research tools and sound advice from start to finish. Sincere thanks also to all the people who provided online accounts of their personal paranormal experiences—their numbers are too great to acknowledge individually. Dennis W. Hauck's *Haunted Places: The National Directory* proved invaluable, as did Rosemary Ellen Guiley's *The Guinness Encyclopedia of Ghosts and Spirits*. Thanks to all of you.

Finally, I'd like to thank my family for giving me the time and space needed to write another book. I couldn't have done it without you.

Introduction

"Are we going to be friends forever?" asked Piglet.
"Even longer," Pooh answered.
> —A.A. Milne, *Winnie the Pooh*

When I was a little girl, I was never lonely. Everywhere I went I had two mysterious friends who accompanied me. Their names, still clear in my memory, were Jamber and Axelmoe. It never occurred to me to wonder about their ages or genders or where they came from. I accepted their presence in the innocent way that only children accept the inexplicable. They just were. I included them in everything I did. I talked to them nonstop. When I fell asleep at night, I was secure in the knowledge that if monsters lurked under my bed or in my closet, they couldn't hurt me: I lay safely between my two otherworldly companions. I don't believe that my invisible playmates were figments of my imagination any more than I believe that the stories in this book are simply the result of the fantastic imaginings of the people who lived them.

When Ghost House Books approached me with the idea of a romantically, instead of a geographically, themed collection of ghost stories, the idea intrigued me. Immediately the movie *Ghost* (1990) with Patrick Swayze came to mind, but as I began to work on the project I realized that finding sources for "romantic" ghost stories would be more challenging than I had initially thought.

The reason, I soon discovered, was simple: most of the earthbound spirits that attach themselves to a person or to a place do so out of a tragic sense of confusion or unhappiness. People who have experienced fulfilling and loving relationships during their mortal lives usually undergo a smooth and uneventful passing into the next world. Of course, there are incidents in which spirits will return to warn loved ones of danger or reassure them of their well-being, as in some of the following stories. More common, however, are tales involving the brokenhearted, the betrayed and the deceived, who haunt the people or the places they have left behind. It is only when their deaths have been avenged, or when justice has been done, that they are able to rest in peace.

In a perfect world there would be no romantic ghost stories. Unfortunately, the world of romantic relationships is flawed, and love can be as unpredictable as the weather. Although many of the stories in this book paint a frightening picture of what can happen when people confuse love with obsession, or loyalty with jealousy, others illustrate the indestructible bond that exists between those lucky enough to have met their soul mates.

1
Star-crossed Spirits

Alice of the Hermitage
NEAR MURRELLS INLET, SOUTH CAROLINA

There are women capable of loving many men and there are women who can love only one. Alice Belin Flagg belonged to the latter group, and as she would discover, it is often those people who suffer the most devastating heartbreaks. Among the wealthy classes in the antebellum South, there was no greater failing for a woman than to fall for a man from a lower class. Those who did suffered humiliation and heartbreak; some, like Alice, even lost their lives. So ingrained is the story of Alice of Hermitage in South Carolina folklore that a novel, *Alice Flagg: The Ghost of the Hermitage,* by Nancy Rhyne, has been written about her intense love affair and her short, tragic life.

In 1849, Alice and her widowed mother lived under the rules of her ambitious brother, Dr. Allard Flagg, in Murrells Inlet at the Hermitage, a vine-draped mansion surrounded on three sides by tidal creeks. The extravagant home suited a powerful plantation owner and his family.

Little was expected of Alice and others like her. As she blossomed from a child into a young woman, her bright personality and alluring good looks began to attract the attentions of many of the most eligible local bachelors. She enjoyed the enviable position of being courted by a string of handsome young men. Her brother went to sleep at night secure in the knowledge that his little sister would marry well and make the family proud. After all, Alice had an easygoing personality and wanted to please her brother.

At the appropriate age, she was presented to society and quickly became a belle of the local scene. From the ages of 14 to 16, Alice lived in a fairy-tale world where her days were spent honing the skills that would one day be required of a rich plantation wife. She learned to play the piano, to dance and to converse. She was often fitted with beautiful ball gowns for the numerous debutante balls she attended in the evenings.

Unfortunately for Alice, the young man who eventually caught her eye was neither wealthy nor sophisticated. He was a handsome, hard-working laborer who was equally smitten by her. Alice's mother tried to talk Alice out of seeing the laborer. She knew the consequences would be dire, and her heart broke for the pain that Alice would have to face if she did not change her mind. But Alice refused to listen. She openly encouraged her suitor. He courted her according to the rules of the South, but nothing could change the fact that he came from a lower echelon of society.

Dr. Allard disapproved of their friendship from the beginning, but when it turned into a full-scale romance, he decided to put an end to it. He forbade Alice to see her young man, but she was a strong-willed girl and she continued to go out with him. Desperate to discourage their liaisons, Dr. Allard shadowed their every move. He refused to acknowledge the young man's presence, and threatened to lock his little sister away in her room.

It was all to no avail. Alice continued to secretly meet with her suitor. The courtship between the young lovers was brief but powerful. They would allow nothing and no one to interfere with their love for each other. Their moments together were fleeting, but they did manage to meet occasionally, and each meeting only served to strengthen the bond that was developing between them. In a final, desperate attempt to sever their relationship completely, Dr. Allard shipped his sister off to a fashionable, very expensive boarding school in Charleston, South Carolina. Alice had no choice but to obey, but the distance served only to cement her feelings for the man she loved.

Before she was whisked away from the Hermitage, Alice's beau placed an engagement ring on her finger. Alice made no attempt to hide the ring. She wore it openly and proudly, defying her brother's wishes. Her mother begged her to be more discreet, but she would not listen to reason. When Dr. Allard discovered the ring, he flew into a rage. He insisted that she return it to her boyfriend. Alice agreed. She promised to do his bidding and slid the ring off her finger.

In her heart, Alice hated her brother. She would take the ring off, but she swore to herself that it would never leave her person. When nobody was looking, she secretly looped it around her neck on a ribbon. For the duration of her school life it would lay next to her heart, hidden from prying eyes.

Alice was not happy at boarding school. The other girls were kind to her, but she was not interested in new friendships and remained aloof. Although she excelled academically, she could not rid her heart or mind of the man who had sworn to wait for her, forever if necessary. As the weeks rolled into months, Alice became more and more homesick. She slumped around in a trance-like state, and as her appetite dwindled the once-robust girl grew weak and frail. Eventually illness invaded her weakened body.

The school doctor was summoned. He examined Alice carefully. His official diagnosis was malaria. As he looked into his feverish patient's eyes, he intuitively sensed that the young girl was suffering from something much more serious than a physical affliction. It seemed to him that she had no will to live. He wondered what terrible thing had happened to her to make her give up her future. But he kept his thoughts to himself, instead advising the headmistress to send her home; the risk to the other students was too great.

By the time Dr. Allard arrived to take her home, Alice's fever had spiked. He bundled her into his carriage, shocked at the amount of weight she had lost. The journey home was long and the ride uncomfortable. He feared she might die en route. As the hot, humid nights and damp, blistering days passed, Alice's condition worsened. Dr. Allard prayed that his sister would survive the four-day journey. He worried about who would look after her when they got home. Hermitage House was empty in the spring—their mother and most of the servants had retreated to the safety of the South Carolina foothills to escape malaria-carrying mosquitoes. Dr. Allard stayed behind to oversee the plantation.

In spite of the terrible odds, Alice was still alive when they arrived at the Hermitage. The sweet scent of gardenias hung heavily in the air as her brother carried her wasting body through the large veranda and up to her bedroom. As Alice slipped in and out of consciousness, she sought out the ring that hung around her neck, finally pulling it from beneath her nightgown. Dr. Allard was furious when he saw it. Nobody had ever dared to disobey him, yet his waif of a sister continued to do so. He grabbed the simple band of gold out of Alice's hand, deaf to her cries of protest. Then he strode across the room, flung open the nearest window and tossed it into Hermitage Creek.

Alice became agitated and inconsolable. All through the night she wept and pleaded with her brother to go and find her ring. The next morning she died, still crying for her ring. Dr. Allard had no way of reaching their mother. He felt alone and guilty. Unsure of what to do, he decided to bury her body on the grounds of the Hermitage until he could hold a proper service and interment. He dressed her in the same white gown that she had worn at her coming-out ball and laid her out for viewing in a glass coffin. Her pale skin was hardly distinguishable from her virginal white dress. Neighbors and friends arrived from miles around to pay their last respects.

When their mother returned, she ordered that her daughter's body be buried in the cemetery at All Saints Church near Pawley's Island. It was assumed she would rest in peace beneath the giant oaks of South Carolina. As for her fiancé, he disappeared without a trace, never to be heard from again. Perhaps the agony of losing the love of his life so needlessly was more than he could bear. I like to think that they were reunited on the other side, and that the love they were denied in life became theirs in death.

All this happened over 150 years ago, but Alice's spirit, bereft of her fiancé and separated from the symbol of their love, did not find peace. Almost immediately after she was buried, a boy visiting the Hermitage encountered a pale young woman on the staircase. "I asked her name," he complained to his mother, "but she refused to answer me. She seemed sad but very beautiful."

A shiver of apprehension settled on the adults gathered at the breakfast table. "Tell us more about her," the boy's mother asked. His description of the beautiful girl perfectly matched the description of Alice Belin Flagg. That initial appearance was to be the first of many. Over the years, the ghost of Alice became a common sight in and around All Saints Cemetery. Sometimes she sits placidly in the gardens of the Hermitage; at other times she is spotted staring out the window of her bedroom or tiptoeing up the grand staircase. Perhaps her saddest manifestations are when she appears in the graveyard, searching futilely for the ring that her long-lost lover gave to her so many generations ago.

Alice's ghost appears in bare feet, with her white burial gown fluttering around her ankles as her thick, dark hair cascades down her back. She doesn't invoke fear in those who encounter her, but rather sadness at the terrible loss she suffered for giving her heart to a man whom her brother would never endorse. Their vows were so powerful that even in death they would not be broken.

Today visitors can go to the All Saints Cemetery and see Alice's final resting place. Her grave marker is simple—a flat slab of stone with her name etched into the surface. Some might even meet the ghost of Alice face-to-face, still searching for her ring.

The Ghostly Music of Harding College

SEARCY, ARKANSAS

Her name is lost to human memory and her body is dust, but the music she played lives on in the halls of an Arkansas college, even though the girl has been dead for over 70 years. The music was the one thing that provided her with solace and comfort in her loneliest time. Harding College is 50 miles northeast of Little Rock. It is a respected co-ed Christian college that was once the stage for a terrible drama that ended in the death of two students.

"Psychic impression" is the term paranormal investigators use to describe an entity that has lost its life force but continues to perform a repetitive act *ad infinitum*. Think of it as the supernatural resonance of a person long gone. It is more common than you might think.

The young girl responsible for the haunting melodies that are still heard in Harding College was a music student in the 1930s. She fell passionately in love with another student—and he with her. If not for the intervention of fate, they might have spent their lives together, but late one night a terrible car accident cut short the boy's life. The young girl became inconsolable and exiled herself to the third-floor music room. She passed the lonely hours bent over her piano, lost in grief and finding some relief in the ivory keys beneath her fingers.

Her friends and her teachers tried everything to break the spell of sadness imposed on her by the terrible accident, but they were helpless in the face of her despondence. She rarely left her piano, sinking instead into a bottomless pit of sorrow where nobody could reach her.

She died only months after the death of her boyfriend. Everyone was saddened, but no one was surprised. Teachers and students alike attributed her passing to a broken heart. Clearly the young woman couldn't face a future without the person she had given her heart to. It was incomprehensible to her that she could ever love another man. She had passed on, but the emotion she had poured into her piano had left a psychic impression in the third-floor music room. Soon after her death, residents of Harding College began to hear hollow melodies drifting down through the ceiling from the music room. As time passed, college students and teachers became used to the plaintive, disembodied notes. Instead of being afraid, they felt empathy for their former colleague.

Years later the college underwent a large reconstruction. The third story, where the music room had once been, was entirely eliminated, and a two-story structure was built in its place. Everyone thought the ghostly music would disappear in the wreckage of renovation. They were wrong—to this day, the eerie notes of the long-dead pianist echo through the halls of Harding College. The music emanates from a nonexistent third floor, where the echoes of love reverberate from beyond the grave.

"Till Death Do Us Join"
JOHNS ISLAND, SOUTH CAROLINA

Fenwick Hall, on Johns Island, is only 12 minutes and two bridges away from Charleston, South Carolina. Today it is recognized as one of America's most remarkable 18th-century plantations. Stockbroker John Pernell owns the mansion and its surrounding 55 acres, although it sat empty and derelict for years. Pernell has fully and lovingly restored the estate and today it is listed on the National Register of Historic Places. Unfortunately, the 3000 acres that once made up the sprawling plantation have long since fallen victim to time and recent development.

Recently, local historians opposed the construction of a high-density housing project, citing the plantation's rich history as a compelling reason for preservation. The ghosts of Fenwick Hall are probably on the side of the preservationists—after all, some of them have been there for over 200 years.

The seventh Earl of Fenwick, Lord Ripon, purchased the land on Johns Island in the mid-1700s. An eccentric man, he commissioned the construction of a large mansion similar to his ancestral castle in England. Ancient silver maples and gnarly oaks conceal Fenwick Hall from the eyes of the curious. These same majestic trees graced Fenwick Hall long ago, when an army of servants and a battalion of slaves moved about the property under the watchful and sometimes cruel eyes of their masters. The celebrated Fenwick stables turned out some of South Carolina's best bloodlines; in fact, the horses received better care than the indentured workers could ever have imagined.

The Fenwicks were known for their extreme wealth, their fast horses and their beautiful women. In those days of patriarchy, the only difference between good bloodlines in a horse and good bloodlines in a woman was that the horse was worth more money in the long run. The lord of the manor extended his kindness and generosity to those who obeyed his word and met his expectations. Those who didn't please him, regardless of whether they were human or animal, paid dearly.

The earl's daughters knew what was expected of them: chastity, obedience and exquisite manners. Their marriages were intended to improve the family line. Once they'd ful-filled their familial obligations, the young women were per-mitted to disappear into a life of banality and comfort. But the earl's youngest daughter, 17-year-old Ann, saw things differently. She flung off the constraints of her gender and social class and entertained herself exactly as she pleased.

Ann was horse crazy. She spent all her free time in the stables, and perhaps it was inevitable that she should fall in love with Tony, the head groom—and he with her. Tony was handsome, bright and he made Ann laugh, but most importantly he had a wonderful way with horses. Out of a shared love for these noble beasts grew a respect for each other that blossomed into a romance. Neither had any intention of conducting their relationship behind Lord Ripon's back. Still, it must have taken an enormous amount of courage for the teenaged Ann to approach her tyrannical father and ask for permission to marry Tony. She did it with all the optimism of a young girl in love.

The heart-wrenching story of Ann and Tony, two star-crossed lovers, is behind the haunting at Fenwick Hall in South Carolina.

Not surprisingly, her father vehemently refused. But Ann naïvely believed that she could bend his iron will. Her tenacity compelled her to ask her father again and again for his blessing. She refused to hide her love for Tony and could see no reason for her father's objections. After all, she argued, Tony had a good job, he already lived on the estate and they both shared a passion for the thoroughbreds that had made the Fenwick name a legend in the racing world.

Ann underestimated her father's snobbery and overestimated his love for her. Since she had been a little girl, she had received everything she wanted, but this time it was different. It took her a long time, but finally she realized that her father would rather see her die of a broken heart than marry a man below her station in life—even if that was the only man she could ever love.

Ann did not easily abandon her dreams. There was only one thing she wanted in life, and that was to be with Tony. Now she had to figure out how to do it. Tony loved her madly, but sometimes when he was alone, he questioned whether they could ever be together. Lord Fenwick was not an easy man to cross, and Tony was secretly afraid of him. But Ann wasn't. After much thought, she came to the conclusion that she had only two options: obey her father and live in misery or flee the only life she had ever known. To her there was no choice. Ann convinced Tony to elope with her. "Eventually Daddy will forgive us," she promised. "You'll see."

Late one night she crept out of her bedroom, carrying only a small bag of necessary clothes. She moved furtively through the thickly carpeted, elegant halls of the castle and beyond the pillars into the humid night. She ran across the magnificent gardens to the stables where Tony awaited her arrival. He had already tacked up the fastest horse in the stable when Ann fell into his arms. Finally they would begin their lives together. "We haven't got a second to lose," she said. "I could be discovered missing at any time."

She climbed up on the horse behind Tony, and without a glance backward they headed for the marsh. There they hoped to find a boat to the mainland, but none was to be had. They searched until they were exhausted.

Finally, they realized that they would have to wait until daylight. It was too late to turn back. A ramshackle hut on the river's edge seemed the perfect place to stay until morning, and so Tony and Ann spent their first night together in each other's arms. It was everything they had hoped for and more. Ann knew in her heart that she had made the right decision. She knew she could not live without Tony.

Before dawn, Lord Ripon discovered that his daughter had run away. He immediately formed a search party to look for her. Enraged, he vowed to avenge his family name and punish his wayward daughter. But he was not prepared to find her in the arms of her lover when he burst into the riverside shed. Out of his mind with anger, he literally dragged them back to the plantation. No one disobeyed the Earl of Fenwick, certainly not his daughter. Ann, terrified but still defiant, was imprisoned in her bedroom. Tony's punishment was much more severe.

Lord Ripon was furious that his head groom had betrayed him, so he sentenced Tony to death by lynching. Tony was quickly bound, blindfolded and placed in the saddle, with a noose around his neck and the end of the rope secured to a silver maple. Still Lord Ripon was not satisfied. In an unparalleled act of cruelty, he forced Ann out to the garden. She screamed and cried and begged for him to show mercy, but he was beyond reason. Instead he placed a horsewhip in her hand. Ann refused to lash the horse beneath Tony, so her father took her hand and did it with her.

The horse leapt forward. Tony's neck snapped like a twig. As Ann watched his life choke out of him, she crumpled to the ground, her lover's name on her lips. "Tony," she called. "Tony." But Tony had been silenced forever. "Tony," she cried again and fell into a dead faint.

From that terrible day on, she never uttered any other word but his name until the day she died. The trauma of seeing her lover die by her own hand caused something to snap in Ann Fenwick. She never regained her sanity, and death came and took her away soon after.

Since that terrible time, bad luck has plagued the Fenwick Plantation. Lord Ripon's descendents lost the property to the Confederate Army during the Civil War and were forced to leave South Carolina.

Today, the spirits of the lovers continue to haunt Fenwick. They are not alone, however; other spirits have been seen, including a headless horseman. But it is the ghosts of Ann and Tony that are most often heard or seen. Sometimes Ann's spirit is spotted alone. It drifts about the property, calling out Tony's name in a plaintive voice. Sometimes, Tony's spirit joins her and then the two lovers walk silently beneath the silver maples, together in death in a way they could never be in life.

The Hunting Knife
PRESTON COUNTY, WEST VIRGINIA

Did the spirit of Tom Ellis return from the grave to avenge his murder? The police in Preston County, West Virginia, were never able to prove it, but the facts of the case point to the frightening conclusion that he did. After all, it is possible for ghosts to assume physical form and attack the living, especially if the ghost feels that justice has not been served.

Tom Ellis and Jack Clayton were best friends. One of the similar interests they shared was a girl they both fell in love with at the same time. The ensuing rivalry for her attentions resulted in the bitter end of their long friendship. The girl chose Tom to be her husband and Jack reacted badly to the news: he vowed never to set foot in Tom's house or speak to him again. He refused to acknowledge his presence in public and would not tolerate hearing his name spoken by others. Jack Clayton turned into a bitter and hateful man.

Tom missed his oldest friend. He missed their fishing and hunting trips and he missed getting together for beers with Jack on a Saturday night. Although he was happy with his new wife, his life did not feel complete. Mrs. Ellis knew about the situation and it hurt her to see her husband so sad. She determined to repair the friendship and begged Jack to forgive Tom. Because he still loved her, and would do anything she asked, Jack Clayton agreed. Soon the men renewed their friendship, and it appeared that there would be no more trouble.

Did the ghost of Tom Ellis kill his murderer and rival Jack Clayton with a hunting knife?

In the fall they resumed their annual hunting trip. The two men set off into the mountains at dawn, promising to return with fresh game within the week. Tom's wife waved them goodbye, happy in the knowledge that the two men had been able to put the old rivalry behind them once and for all. A week later, Jack returned alone and distressed. Apparently Tom had wandered off on his own and did not return to the camp. Jack spent days searching for him, but could find no trace of his old friend. A search party was immediately dispatched, but Tom could not be found.

Although the police suspected foul play, without a body they could prove nothing against Jack Clayton. The case was closed, and life returned to normal in the small West Virginia town. The next fall, Jack took another friend—whose name is not on record but let's call him Jim—on his hunting trip. They arrived at the camp toward nightfall. It was the first time Jack had returned since Tom's death, and Jim thought he seemed a little spooked. They ate a quick meal and then went right to bed. In the dead of the night, Jim awoke to hear Jack screaming, "Don't do it, Tom! Please, don't do it. Leave me alone!"

He leapt out of bed, found a light and discovered Jack Clayton lying in a pool of blood face-up on the cabin floor. A glinting hunting knife protruded from his heart. He guessed by the look on Jack's face that if he hadn't died from the knife wound, he would have died from fright. For a full year, Jim was the main suspect in Jack's murder, but when the snow melted and the investigators and their search dogs returned to the scene of the crime, they found Tom Ellis' body buried in a shallow grave near the camp.

He had been dead for two years. The murder weapon was identified as the knife that had once belonged to the deceased Jack Clayton. Tom had been fatally stabbed once through the heart, and the knife remained embedded in his chest. No charges were ever laid. It was assumed the victim had taken care of the punishment the year before.

Alexander Dunsmuir
SAN FRANCISCO, CALIFORNIA

The Dunsmuir family of Victoria, British Columbia, amassed incredible amounts of wealth in the coal industry during the 1800s. They appeared to lack for nothing, and materially they didn't. What most of their friends and acquaintances failed to realize was that the family was bankrupt emotionally. The elder generation of Dunsmuir ruled over their children with an iron fist. The unspoken rule in their home was that obedience was awarded with cash, and that disobedience meant poverty. But for Alexander, in particular, a deeply ingrained sense of entitlement made it impossible for him to imagine surviving without a hefty income from his parents. It would take a strong person to walk away from it all, and Alexander was weak.

Alexander was the heir to the Dunsmuir fortune, but being born into such wealth carried with it both incredible freedom and terrible repression. Like many sons and daughters of the super-rich, he realized at a young age that his inheritance was directly tied to his lifestyle. Simply put, if he were to inherit any of his family's wealth, he would have to conduct himself according to the values his parents espoused.

These values, remnants from the Victorian era, dictated that a young man would marry a girl from an approved family, and Alexander planned to do just that. Luckily there were plenty of debutantes to choose from, and Alexander was considered an excellent catch by all of them. But Cupid had different plans for the young man, whose nature was ultimately more romantic than practical. By 1878, Alexander had moved to San Francisco and was generally enjoying life as one of the city's most eligible bachelors. At one spirited soirée he met Josephine Wallace. It was love at first sight—a powerful, all-consuming love that he could not control, but also a love that his parents could never condone.

Josephine Wallace was not the ideal woman for Alexander. She was neither virginal nor available. She was married, albeit unhappily, to a man named Weller Wallace when Alexander entered her life. She immediately recognized the newcomer from Canada as her soul mate. To their credit, they both struggled to repress their feelings for each other, but it was like trying to alter the flow of a river—well-nigh impossible. Inevitably they ended up in each other's arms and so began a passionate affair that eventually led to Josephine's divorce from her husband.

Finally the lovers were free to marry. Now that he was no longer required to conceal his love, Alexander knew true happiness. Sadly, his joy was short-lived. Opposition to their union was vicious and immediate. Their Nob Hill friends sided with Weller Wallace, shunning Josephine and her lover, and blaming Alexander for destroying what they saw as a perfectly workable marriage. Blinded by their love for each other and confident that the gossips would soon find someone or something else to target, they went ahead and began planning their wedding.

Alexander forgot to factor his overbearing mother into the picture. When word of her son's matrimonial plans reached her, she was outraged. Alexander was ordered home. He reassured Josephine that she should not worry. He promised her that, with a little persuasion, he could succeed in convincing his mother that she was the only woman for him.

Mrs. Dunsmuir listened to her son's pleas with pursed lips and knuckles clenched. When Alexander had finished, she stood and looked him squarely in the eye. "If you marry this divorcée," she said, "you will be disinherited. You will be disowned. You will have nothing."

Alexander was prepared for everything but that. The threat of being poor, which had hung over his head since he was a little boy, was too much for him to bear. He capitulated to his mother's demands and he promised not to wed Josephine.

Josephine was heartbroken when Alexander returned to San Francisco and broke off the engagement. They decided never to see each other again, but neither could fight the magnetism that had drawn them together in the first place. Surrendering to their love, they moved into a house together and began a semi-secret cohabitation that was to last for 20 years. Former friends ostracized the couple, but nothing, not even the terrible social stigma surrounding their scandalous relationship, affected them. But as the years passed, the isolation they suffered became more and more difficult to bear. Alexander turned to liquor to assuage his unhappiness, but in spite of it all their love remained strong and constant.

When Alexander's controlling mother died, he received his inheritance. For the first time in his life, Alexander didn't have to answer to anyone. After nearly a quarter of a century of living in sin, Josephine and

Alexander exchanged their wedding vows. Alexander's gift to his new bride was to build a new home that they could finally share together openly. He chose prestigious Oakland Hills for the enormous, 16,000-square-foot, 37-room mansion. It sat in the middle of 50 acres, and the gardens were to be the most beautiful in San Francisco. It seemed that Josephine and Alexander could finally revel in the happiness that had evaded them for so long.

While their home was being completed, the newly-weds set off for a much-anticipated honeymoon in New York City. But there was a cloud on the horizon of their happiness.

Alexander had paid a heavy price for the years he'd spent defying his mother. He was losing his battle with alcoholism. Not even his newfound bliss could keep him from the bottle, and the abuse had begun to take a toll on his body.

While in New York, Josephine became seriously ill. She was rushed to hospital and while Alexander waited nervously for the news, he fortified himself with sips from the silver flask he always carried in his pocket. Although he knew as soon as he saw the doctor's face that the diagnosis was serious, nothing prepared him for the shock he felt when he heard the word "cancer." The medical team recommended an immediate operation for Josephine, but within days of the devastating news, Alexander himself, grief stricken and terrified, died of alcohol-induced meningitis.

Bereft, Josephine refused the operation. Instead she returned to San Francisco as Mrs. Alexander Dunsmuir, widow. Alexander also returned, but he was in a coffin.

Josephine Dunsmuir left her lavish home in Oakland after the unexpected death of her beloved husband, Alexander.

Josephine had his body interred at Mountainview Cemetery. Their mansion in Oakland Hills had been completed, but Josephine had no desire to live in it without the man she had loved. She fled San Francisco, where she had never been made to feel welcome, and went north to Victoria, where she moved in with her brother-in-law, James, and his family.

In her grief, all thoughts of her own health were forgotten. James did his best to make her comfortable, but Josephine's thoughts were with the dead, not the living. She ached for Alexander, and thought only of him day and night.

Alexander must have heard her painful cries. One evening, as she sat, head bowed, wondering how she could get through yet another day without him, she heard her name. "Josephine." She knew his voice. Afraid to look up, in case it might not be true, she took a big breath and lifted her eyes. There in front of her, as large and real as life, stood Alexander. He smiled lovingly and began to speak. "Go to the doctor and have your operation, my dear," he said. "If you delay any longer, you will not live, and it is not your time yet. I will wait for you. I love you."

Josephine felt a great sense of relief. She had proof that the man she'd loved for so many years still existed—not in her world, but somewhere. She departed for New York immediately and underwent the operation. She survived her husband by only a year, but went to her own death secure in the knowledge that her soul mate awaited her on the other side.

The Ghost of Francis Rattenbury
VICTORIA, BRITISH COLUMBIA

Alma Rattenbury ran the sharp blade of the carving knife over her palm, drawing a line of bright red blood in the soft skin. It didn't hurt much, but that didn't surprise her—she felt nothing anymore. Numbness had become her state of mind. It was peaceful here on the banks of the river, she thought—as good a place to die as any.

She raised the knife, the handle bloodied from her own hand, and plunged it into her breast. Once to remember her first husband (she winced at that thought), a second time for number two (she should be getting used to it now) and a third for poor Francis, whose death she had brought on. The fourth strike pierced her heart and she thought about George, who sat on death row (he had been loyal to the end). The fifth strike also pierced her heart and she slumped to the ground, using the last of her energy to stick the knife into her chest one last time. They found her that way, lying in her own blood on the banks of the Avon River, with six deep knife wounds in her chest. In these actions of violence against herself, she managed to save the life of her lover. George Percy Stoner's death sentence was commuted and he served only seven years in prison, securing his release before he reached the age of 30.

Alma died in England in June 1935, but her story begins across the ocean in Kamloops, British Columbia, almost 40 years earlier, where she was born to a simple printer and his wife. Alma was a beautiful child and she grew into a stunning woman who used her incredible beauty and allure to exploit men. She was in her late 20s and had already been married and divorced twice when she met the well-known architect Francis Rattenbury. He had designed every single important building in Victoria, B.C., as well as the Royal London Wax Museum and the Vancouver Art Gallery.

Francis was born in England in 1867 and immigrated to Victoria in 1891. Strangely, it is *his* ghost that haunts the city he designed, while Alma's spirit rests in peace far from the land where she was born. Both were guilty of betrayal, but only Alma died with her own blood and that of others on her hands.

Although Francis came from a long line of architects, he had little experience when he won the contract to design Victoria's Legislature Buildings. Overnight he became a wealthy man, and his next commission, to design the Empress Hotel (now the Fairmont Empress Hotel), secured his position in the crème de la crème of Victoria's predominantly British society. He married Florence Nunn and they had two children. They appeared to be a happy family, until Alma arrived on the scene. The first time Francis saw her, he lost his heart. She had a job playing the piano in the lobby of the Empress Hotel. They soon became embroiled in a passionate love affair. It was not an accident that Francis Rattenbury noticed Alma Pakenham. If Alma wanted a man, Alma got him—she just made sure that he thought it was his idea.

Within two years, Francis and Florence were divorced and Alma became the new Mrs. Rattenbury. The former Mrs. Rattenbury died—some say of a broken heart. But Francis' illicit liaison with Alma while he was still married effectively destroyed his reputation in Victoria. Suddenly out of work, he decided, reluctantly, to move back to England to open an architectural firm in his native country. The loss of business and the move exerted a heavy financial toll on him, but he was willing to do anything for his new bride and their baby son.

They chose Bournemouth, a small resort town on the coast where Francis thought there would be plenty of opportunity for an experienced architect with a magnificent portfolio. Starting over proved more difficult than he had imagined. Alma had little tolerance for a poor husband, and soon her love for him turned to disdain. Defeated, Francis accepted his wife's contempt with little protest, turning instead to liquor for comfort.

Alma recognized that her husband's alcohol-induced lethargy offered her the chance to find a more suitable lover. She penned an advertisement in the local paper requesting the services of a live-in houseboy who would be no older than 18 years old, strong and helpful. She cared little about his level of education or references. She had other things on her mind.

George Percy Stoner was the perfect fit. He applied for the position and she hired him immediately. Within months, George was a regular visitor to Alma's bed. As their attraction for each other developed, Alma became bolder with her houseboy, seemingly repeating the pattern that Francis had begun with her while poor dead Florence still lived.

A clandestine weekend in London sealed their union, making it impossible to continue to co-exist under the same roof as Francis. George's love for Alma bordered on obsession, and Alma relished the attention she received from him, even if she didn't love him.

A week later, on March 24, 1935, Mr. and Mrs. Rattenbury and their chauffeur/houseboy were overnight guests at the home of a business prospect of the architect's. That evening, Alma bade Francis good night and retired. Soon after, as was their habit, George joined her. Some time later, a doctor was summoned to the home. He found Rattenbury slumped in his chair, one side of his head a bloody pulp, barely alive. Alma was drunk and semi-hysterical, while George was quiet and helpful. George and the doctor rushed Francis to the hospital where he died without regaining consciousness.

Alma and Francis Rattenbury during happier times; Alma later murdered her husband with the help of her lover.

The next day Alma and her houseboy were arrested and charged with first-degree murder. Alma, high on morphine that the doctor had given her to calm her nerves, confessed. She later recanted, blaming the murder on George. George did not defend himself. He insisted that he was guilty and his lover was innocent.

The trial caused a sensation in both England and Canada. Although Alma was found innocent, the judge admonished her for corrupting a boy less than half her age, bringing in evidence that constant sexual relations with a man so young was "unnatural and harmful" to his health and well-being.

George Percy Stoner received the death sentence. Alma was released into a world where not even her family accepted her. The details of her physical relationship with her houseboy offended and disgusted almost everyone.

It is probable that the truth of what happened on the night of her husband's murder had more to do with Alma than with George. Her journal entries following George's sentencing show a woman racked with guilt—the same guilt that led her to the banks of the Avon River and to a suicide designed to save the life of the boy who had been willing to sacrifice his own for hers.

And what of Francis Rattenbury? In Victoria's quaint capital, tourists may stroll down a street named after him, or wander through the many regal structures that he designed. It is also possible to meet him face-to-face, for his spirit still wanders the halls of the Fairmont Empress Hotel—his favorite project and the place where he once knew real happiness. Hotel employees are familiar with Francis and allow him a peaceful existence.

John and Mary
EDISTO ISLAND, SOUTH CAROLINA

The coast of the Carolinas is dotted with tiny islands rich in history. Today they are a vacationer's paradise, and tourists who visit them often return summer after summer to relax in the warm southern sun and soak up the many stories. But on beautiful Edisto Island on the coast of South Carolina, sinister forces lurk behind the beautiful surroundings.

The history of the island is mired in sadness. Death was not uncommon in this tiny paradise, which was named for its original inhabitants, the Edistow tribe. Most of the tribe had been decimated by smallpox in the early

1700s, and those who survived were eventually wiped off the face of the earth by other illnesses. All the locals knew that the ghosts of these people frequented the island.

The Europeans, who brought disease to the indigenous peoples of Edisto, soon colonized the island. It quickly became a summer playground for rich plantation families. In the heavy heat of the southern months, they would abandon their mainland mansions for the cool sea breezes that blew in off the Atlantic. Many spent from July to September in the small beach houses that dotted the coastline, far from the threat of malaria, since mosquitoes are less plentiful near the ocean.

John Fickling and Mary Clark were both born on Edisto Island and came from wealthy families. They spent their childhoods together playing on the sandy beaches, and as they grew into adulthood their friendship blossomed into a romance. It seemed natural that they would one day marry, so neither their friends nor their families were surprised when John Fickling asked Miss Mary Clark to be his wife. She accepted without hesitation. After all, it was difficult for either of them to imagine what life might be like without each other.

The couple married in the spring in St. Stephens Church. The wedding feast took place on the beach, where they and their guests stayed up until dawn, enjoying the music, food and an air of festivity. Every toast to the bride and groom reaffirmed the overwhelming strength of their union. Nobody doubted that John and the new Mrs. Fickling would be anything but happy together. The guests were correct—the Ficklings quickly settled into married life and grew even closer to each other.

John Fickling was a sea captain, so he spent much of his time away from home. Mary hated it when he left and was always anxious until he came home. Soon after their wedding he had to go to sea. Mary stood on the beach and waved goodbye to her new husband. He was bound for the West Indies, his ship laden with cotton and wood. It was a journey he had made many times before, but for some reason, Mary felt uneasy about his departure this time. She blew him a kiss and waited until his schooner was entirely out of sight, then she turned and walked slowly across the sand back to their home. She knew he would be gone for at least three months, and the days stretched emptily before her.

Mary had a lot to do while John was gone. They were in the middle of setting up their new home and she had her family and many friends to support her and keep her occupied. Every night, before she fell asleep, she prayed for her husband's safe passage. Still, the summer seemed to go on forever. As the day of John's return neared, Mary could hardly contain her excitement.

Schooner arrival dates in those days were not predictable, and the due date passed without any sign of John's ship in the waters off Edisto Island. Every day Mary went down to the shoreline to watch for him, and every night she returned home disappointed. She fought back a growing sense of dread in the pit of her stomach. October approached, bringing with it the threat of wild hurricanes, and Mary grew more and more concerned.

One morning Mary awoke suddenly. She hurried out of bed and down to the beach. She searched the water for some sign of John, but the horizon was empty and the sea was dead flat. She had grown up on Edisto, and nobody had to tell her that a storm was on its way. Hours later, the hurricane struck. It was as savage and merciless as anyone on the Carolina coast could remember. It raged for a day and a night, leaving in its wake destroyed buildings, ruined crops and shattered lives. Waves four stories high pounded the coastline and the winds carried off barns, farm equipment and furniture. Mary and her family were prisoners in their home until the howling wind and driving rain abated.

As quickly as it had arrived, the hurricane subsided. The water returned to an eerie calm. As the residents calculated their terrible losses, they struggled to comprehend the raw power of nature. The sun returned as suddenly as it had disappeared and they began to clean up.

Mary Fickling had spent the past day begging God to deliver her husband home. The morning after the storm, she set off alone to walk along Edingsville Beach. She was determined that she would be the first person he saw upon his arrival. She picked her way through the remnants of the storm, recognizing bits of houses, roofing, clothing, chairs and other household items scattered over the sand.

Please come home to me, John, she prayed, scanning the vacant horizon for the slightest movement. Suddenly, out of the corner of her eye, she spotted a movement in the tide line. From afar it was difficult to tell what it was. She moved closer to it. It floated lazily in the green water and she thought it looked vaguely familiar. Then it dawned on her. It seemed to be a human form. She hiked up her skirt and waded into the ocean. The closer she got, the sicker she felt. Finally she was close enough to touch the body. It floated face-down as she reached out and turned it over. John, her precious John, stared up her. She pulled the lifeless body of her husband into her shaking arms, praying for a miracle, but there was none.

Mary's prayers had been answered. John had returned to his beloved wife. His schooner and his crew were lost at sea, victims of the hurricane, and were never seen again.

Today, not much remains of Edisto. The eroding power of the sea over the ages has changed the shape of Edisto Island. Locals say that whenever a hurricane has blown through, the spirit of Mary Fickling revisits her home. On these occasions, her lonesome figure is seen on the beach reclaiming the body of her husband from the Atlantic. She pulls him up onto the beach, settles down beside him and wraps her small arms around his cold, wet body.

The Bridal Chamber
SILVER SPRINGS RIVER, FLORIDA

Every year, thousands of visitors are attracted to lush
north-central Florida. Its intricate system of inland water-
ways spread across the state like a fine spider web of rivers,
streams and creeks. One of the major water features is
Silver Springs River, which feeds into the world's largest
artesian springs. Here, over 100 years ago, Claire Douglass
and Bernice Mayo lived out a classic Romeo-and-Juliet
drama of love and suicide. Today their ghosts remain forever locked 30 feet beneath the clear waters of Silver
Springs' Bridal Chamber.

Claire was the only child of wealthy landowner
Captain Harding Douglass. Bernice was the daughter of
Tom and Jessie Lee Mayo, dirt-poor sharecroppers who
worked from dawn until dusk on the Douglass land to put
food on their table. While the Mayos struggled daily to
eke out a subsistence living, Claire lived a lonely life of
privilege. He was a quiet, solemn child who dreamed of a
different life—a life in which he had siblings and a mother
to care for him. He didn't understand why his mother had
abandoned him. He heard that she had fled her husband's
terrible temper immediately after his birth, leaving Claire
with a hastily scrawled note that read "Remember, I'll love
you always. Mother." Beside it she had placed a golden
bracelet embedded with blood-red rubies and ivory-white
pearls. The bracelet became Claire's most precious possession—the only tangible memory he had of her. He carried
it with him everywhere.

Captain Douglass' cruelty extended beyond the treatment of his wife. He hardly spoke to Claire and when he did, it was to heap criticism or insults on his only son. Every year Claire's dislike and fear of his father increased, until even being in the same room with him made him feel sick and helpless. The sharecroppers who worked the land hated and feared him, and Bernice's family had particular reason to despise the cruel-hearted man. When Bernice was only two years old, she suddenly became deathly ill. In desperation, her mother went up to the main house and humbly begged Captain Douglass to provide medicine to cure her baby. She did not have enough money to buy it herself and she feared her little girl might die. Captain Douglass bluntly turned down her request. In his mind, the sharecroppers already had too many children. Losing one meant one less mouth to feed, as far as he was concerned.

Bernice's mother left the Douglass house with a heavy heart, certain that she was about to lose her baby. Unable to face her family right away, she decided to go for a walk by the water. On the shores of Silver Springs there lived an ageless black healer known to everyone simply as Aunt Silla. She overheard Bernice's mother crying softly. She listened to her story then she shook her head, looked at her wisely and said, "Tears ain't gonna help nothing." Aunt Silla asked if she could take Bernice to stay with her in her cabin by the river. She promised she would return her to her family in good health. Bernice's mother was willing to try anything at this point, so she agreed, although she had almost given up hope.

Aunt Silla kept her word. For almost a week little Bernice stayed with the healer and at the end of that time, she was completely cured. Not only that, a life-long bond formed between Bernice and the woman who had brought her back from the brink of death. From that time on, the medicine woman took a special interest in Bernice. She promised to read her fortune, and when Bernice was a young teenager, she looked into her future and smiled. She foresaw that Bernice was destined to fall in love with a wealthy young man who would always cherish her.

So it was that Aunt Silla showed no surprise when Claire Douglass and Bernice Mayo fell in love. Claire's father reacted completely differently. He flew into a rage. He swore that no son of his would ever marry a share-cropper's daughter. It would bring shame upon the family name. His fury fell on deaf ears. Claire loved Bernice. Her impoverished background meant nothing to him, and the more his father ordered him not to see her, the more determined he became to follow his heart. Claire had been lonely for too long to give up the girl he loved and who loved him.

Captain Douglass was stubborn man. He enlisted the help of Claire's embittered spinster aunt. At her brother's request, she whisked Claire off to Europe, determined to make him either change his mind or forget Bernice altogether. Claire went unwillingly, but not before he had promised himself to Bernice. "Don't worry," he reassured her, "my heart belongs to you and nobody else. I promise to always love you. Wait for me." To seal his oath of love, he gave her his most treasured possession—his mother's golden bracelet. She placed it on her wrist and swore never to remove it. As soon as Claire and his aunt left the country, Captain Douglass evicted the Mayo family.

Bernice and Claire made many attempts to exchange letters while he was away, but unbeknownst to the lovers, Claire's father and aunt intercepted all their mail. Time passed, and when Claire didn't hear from Bernice, he assumed she'd forgotten him, or worse yet, betrayed him. Bernice arrived at a similar conclusion, but for her it would prove fatal—the brokenhearted girl willed herself to die, unable to face a future without Claire. There was nothing anybody could do to stop her. Because she and Claire had spent countless happy hours together at Aunt Silla's cabin, Bernice chose to die there, surrounded by her happy memories.

Aunt Silla possessed vast powers, but she could not heal a broken heart. Bernice lay in the small shack on the shore of the springs, her eyes fixed on the bracelet Claire had given her. She refused food and drink, and said little. The medicine woman's powers were useless against Bernice's will. She grew pale and weak until finally she confided in her friend that she had a terrible dread of being buried in the ground. "You must take my body," said Bernice, "to Silver Springs and put it in the water there. If you love me, you will carry out my wish. Please, dear Aunt Silla." Those were her last words. Bernice closed her eyes and passed into the next world.

Months later, Claire returned home to the plantation. He had thought of nothing but Bernice while he had been away and he burned with curiosity to know why she had not answered any of his letters. When he arrived home, his father informed him that he would soon marry the daughter of a wealthy friend. Heavy with sadness and unable to fight anymore, Claire agreed. As soon as he could, he sought out Aunt Silla. Perhaps she could tell him what had become of Bernice. He discovered the woman sitting on her rickety porch. She looked older than he remembered. Her skin sagged and she had lost all the vitality that he remembered so well. She sat as still as death and there was a vacant look in her once-bright eyes. He touched her shoulder, but she didn't respond. "Please tell me where Bernice is," he begged. She pointed toward Silver Springs River. Claire could get no more out of her. Clearly she had lost her mind and was making no sense. He shrugged and walked down to the water's edge.

Claire launched the boat—the same boat that he and Bernice had spent endless joyful hours in together. He rowed out to the spot above Silver Springs where he had proposed to Bernice. It all seemed such a long time ago. Still convinced that Bernice had left him for another man, he let his mind drift backward, unable to understand how she could have done this to him. He felt frightened and more alone than he had ever felt in his whole life. He regretted giving her his mother's gold bracelet. Lost in his thoughts, he let the small boat drift in the clear waters. He must somehow learn to forget Bernice. A lump formed in his throat and he leaned over the side of the boat to dip his hand in the cool water. A glint of gold, a reflection from the deep flashed in the pool. The object was vaguely familiar. He looked more closely. A girl's pale arm moved gently in the current below him. He recognized his mother's bracelet. He recognized Bernice's image, blurred by the gently moving waters. Suddenly it became clear to Claire that he had been wrong—that Bernice had never meant to leave him, that she had sacrificed her life for him.

When visitors to Silver Springs River look through their glass-bottomed boats, they might see the ethereal forms of two dead lovers.

Claire knew what he had to do and did not hesitate. He leapt from the boat and sank until his fingers touched Bernice's soft hand. He pulled, hoping to release her, but her body was wedged between two boulders. Claire pulled himself close to her. He inhaled. As the crystal waters filled his lungs, he welcomed death.

Minutes later, Aunt Silla came out of her trance. She looked toward the Silver Springs where the empty boat floated. She smiled. The lovers were together at last.

Their location on Silver Springs River is now called the "Bridal Chamber." Tourists who pass over the watery grave in glass-bottomed boats are warned to avert their eyes unless they are prepared to glimpse the ethereal forms of Claire and Bernice locked in each other's arms for eternity. Although their time on earth was tragically cut short, those who see them entwined together forever can be comforted by the fact that the ties that once bound them in this world are now unbreakable.

"I'll Wait for You"
FORT BRIDGER, WYOMING

The vow, "until death do us part," is often omitted from 21st-century marriage ceremonies by couples who have carefully weighed reality against idealism. These people strive for a truth they can live with. With divorce rates soaring over 50 percent, and with many people choosing not to marry at all, the phrase might seem unrealistic to some. Perhaps that is why an increasingly cynical public swallows up real-life stories of successful marriages. The following story is for those of you who might need to be reminded that for some lucky men and women, love can be everlasting, even beyond the grave.

The historic Fort Bridger Cemetery is located in the southwestern corner of the state of Wyoming. In 1987, the ghost of an elderly gentleman was first spotted drifting through the graveyard, as if searching for somebody or something that he was not able to find on the other side. Described as a tall, gray-haired man wearing a white cowboy hat, he seemed particularly fond of trailing the groundskeeper, Ramon Arthur, around the cemetery, showing a curiosity in newly dug burial plots. The groundskeeper tolerated his presence without fear.

He seemed familiar to the groundskeeper, who eventually recognized the ghost. Ramon also knew that the ghost's aging widow, who missed him terribly, still lived in Fort Bridger. This spirit had learned an important lesson in his marriage: women sometimes take longer than men to get ready, and there is nothing that can be done about it.

Their marriage had been a long and happy one. They had been the best of friends and had cemented their bond with a healthy dose of respect, compromise and mutual understanding. The widow missed her husband terribly. Perhaps she would have been comforted if she had known that he was waiting for her on the other side.

The following year, in 1988, his patience was repaid and his wife died. With her passing, all sightings of the elderly man in the cowboy hat ceased. Incredibly, it appeared that the ghost had chosen to remain in limbo until his beloved wife of many years could join him. For this couple, death parted them only temporarily: their love endured throughout life and beyond.

The Golden North Hotel
SKAGWAY, ALASKA

Gold! The very utterance of the word turned practical men into dreamers. With a little luck and some hard work, even the poorest person had a shot at unimaginable riches. Klondike Ike was one of those men. When word of a massive gold strike in the Yukon reached him in Skagway, Alaska, he joined the thousands of hopeful prospectors heading north by any means possible over the hostile White Pass.

Undaunted by freezing temperatures, terrible storms, driving sleet and nearly impassable ice fields, he set off, convinced he would return a rich man. The night before he left Skagway, he said farewell to his girlfriend Mary, and swore that he would come back for her as soon as he'd staked a claim. But an avalanche en route buried him thousands of feet beneath cement-hard snow, and his promise to Mary could not be fulfilled.

As the months of waiting turned into a year, Mary refused to believe that Ike would not keep his word to her. Every single day, she waited for his arrival, alone in her small room on the top floor of the Golden North Hotel. The locals of Skagway became accustomed to her sad, expectant face staring out at Skagway's Main Street and busy harbor between slightly parted curtains.

As hope for Ike's return dwindled, Mary grew thinner and quieter. Soon she couldn't bear to leave her room, and her subsequent death from pneumonia surprised no one. Mary had choked to death on her own bodily fluids, still believing that Ike lived and had neglected to keep his promise to her. When word of Ike's death at last reached Skagway, people hoped that Mary had finally got her wish and that she and her lover were together again on the other side. Somehow that never happened. Mary's reluctance to give up her vigil for Ike prevented her spirit from leaving her room in the Golden North Hotel. Soon after her passing, her ghost was spotted peering out of her third-story window.

Today, over 100 years later, Skagway has become a destination stop for the cruise ships that sail along North America's spectacular West Coast. Every year, thousands of tourists disembark in Skagway. Many of them are greeted by a slender girl who stares mournfully out at the harbor. Those who know the legend of Mary and Klondike Ike often reserve room 23 at the Golden North Hotel, in hopes of meeting the girl who still waits for a promise to be fulfilled. Mary has been known to choke unwary guests, in a frightening reenactment of her own painful death.

Reports of sightings of Mary's ghost are frequent. Both the hotel's proprietors and many guests have seen the wide-eyed, seemingly sweet girl who wanders the plush halls and rooms in a long white dress. Unexplainable noises, chandeliers that swing and a ghostly apparition merely cause curiosity, but when Mary's unhappy ghost climbed into bed with a newlywed couple, and when she made several attempts to strangle guests, a decision was made to call in a team of exorcists. They were unsuccessful in their efforts to rid the Golden North Hotel of Ike's ethereal girlfriend. Some well-meaning guests have also

A sad story of the gold rush era contributes to the paranormal activity at the Golden North Hotel in Skagway, Alaska.

tried to persuade sad Mary to sever her earthly ties, but she has not listened.

In the 1980s, Donna and Dave Whitehead purchased the Skagway landmark and restored the hotel to its original splendor. Skeptical at first about their resident ghost, they soon became believers in the paranormal. Mary never caused any harm or fright to the Whiteheads or their children, but she also made sure they were aware of her ghostly presence. They have accepted her as one of their family, but no one has been able to offer an explanation for the strange blue orb that hovers occasionally in room 14. Could it be that Klondike Ike also lives in the Golden North Hotel?

2
Fatal Attraction

The Headless Husband
MANNINGTON, WEST VIRGINIA

For the most part, murder victims tend to return to haunt the place of the death more often than those who have died of natural causes—especially if the crime has never been solved and justice has not been served. Although dismemberment does not always prevent a successful passing over from life into death, in many cases hauntings seem to occur even more frequently when a murder victim has suffered the loss of a limb or the head. There are many ghost stories, such as the one below, that involve spirits returning to find their missing appendages.

Willie Jones, of Freeland's Hollow near Mannington, West Virginia, did not deserve the fate that awaited him when he turned his amorous attentions to Helen Morgan. Little did he know that he would become entangled in a love triangle that would end with his tragic death.

The citizens of Freeland's Hollow were simple people who lived together in a tight-knit community where hard work was rewarded with church socials, dinners and similar events. At these gatherings, the young people could mingle under the watchful eyes of their elders. Helen Morgan did not have to worry about finding a future husband for herself. Pretty and well liked, she was actively pursued by the young men of Freeland's Hollow. There were two in particular who sought her attentions. She liked both of them, and encouraged them equally.

George Gump and Willie Jones began courting Helen Morgan at the same time. What began as a friendly rivalry quickly turned into something much uglier. Helen took her time deciding which of the two young men she chose to be her husband. In the callous or perhaps naïve manner of young women who don't have to put any effort into being popular, Helen exercised her right to fickleness. She happily alternated between the two men, attending spelling bees with George, picnics with Willie and giving both the impréssion that he was the special person in her life.

Eventually Willie's exasperation at her flirtatiousness erupted and he demanded that Helen choose between himself and George. After much indecision, because she really liked them both, she chose Willie. She liked that he knew what he wanted and had shown the courage to ask her to make a choice. George took the news badly and did everything in his power to change Helen's mind. He begged her to marry him or at least to give him a second chance at courting her, but she turned a deaf ear on his pleas. The more he asked, the less she respected him. She and Willie married that spring.

While the newlyweds were exchanging their vows in front of the community, George Gump hid in the forest and swore an oath of his own—that he would exact revenge upon Willie Jones—the man who, in his eyes, had ruined his life and shattered his romantic dreams. In his irrational frame of mind, it never occurred to him that Helen did not want him. He blamed the whole situation on Willie.

Helen and Willie settled into married life easily. If Helen missed the excitement of courtship, she was content with the security that came with living with a new husband who adored her. When she discovered she was pregnant, she told Willie and their happiness was complete. But when George heard the news, he sunk into a deep depression. Out of his mind with jealousy, he began to plot the end of his rival's life. At first it was just fantasy, but the more he thought about it, the more attractive the idea became to him.

As her pregnancy progressed and Helen's figure changed, Willie decided that the next time he went into town, he would surprise his wife and buy her the best material he could find so that she could have a new gingham dress that she could wear comfortably throughout the summer months. He set off early one morning in his wagon and spent the day doing chores. Finally, when his wagon was loaded up with supplies, he allowed himself a stop at the local saloon where he spent the evening drinking with friends he hadn't seen for a long time. At midnight, slightly inebriated, he climbed into his wagon and urged his horses forward down the dark road toward home and his pregnant wife. The roll of gingham was tucked up beside him on the bench. He couldn't wait to see Helen's face when she saw the new material he had purchased for her.

A few miles out of town, George Gump, crazed with jealousy, waited for the arrival of the man he had sworn revenge upon. The right moment had finally arrived. There was no one else on the road and it was dark. Willie's heavily laden wagon rattled down the dirt track. As it passed him, George leapt from his hiding place in the shadows. He jumped Willie from behind and stabbed him to death. But the enraged George did not stop at murder.

In a fit of passion he hacked off Willie's head. When he was finished he was covered in blood and shaking all over. In some ways it felt like he had just awoken from a dream. He carefully retrieved Willie's head, which had rolled beneath the wagon and left it beside his battered body. Willie's glassy, dead eyes stared up at him accusingly. The gingham material, now bloodied and ruined, acted as a cushion for his rival's head. *I'm sorry,* George thought, *but you deserved it. Now neither one of us can have Helen.*

The discovery of Willie's headless body the next day repulsed the small community of Freeland's Hollow. Everyone knew who the killer was, but George Gump had disappeared without a trace. He was never seen again and so his crime went unpunished. Perhaps that is why the spirit of Willie Jones revisits the scene of his brutal murder once a month on a full moon. His headless ghost urges his horses through the dark night. Beside him the bolt of gingham sits on the bench. Willie is still trying to deliver it to the wife he loved so much but would never see again in the earthly realm.

An unresolved crime is often all it takes to bring murder victims back to relive again and again the terror of their death. Only after justice has been served will the ghosts pass easily over to the other side.

Lady Marion
LUDLOW CASTLE, ENGLAND

The thick stone walls of Ludlow Castle have borne witness to treachery, murder and heartbreak. Between the 12th and 15th centuries, inhabitants of the castle indulged in murderous plots to overthrow various members of the royal family. Built as a defensive castle along the Welsh-English border by the ambitious Walter de Lacy, who had been second in command to William the Conqueror, the structure is steeped in bloodshed and brutality. It is perched ominously on the high ground between the Teme and the Corve Rivers—a sprawling, magnificent reminder of a past in which death lurked around every corner and one never knew who was a friend and who was an enemy.

It is not surprising that Ludlow Castle harbors a host of apparitions. Prince Arthur's heart is buried on the castle grounds, and the doomed royal princes, Edward and Richard, spent their childhood under the shadows of Ludlow's towers.

Visitors who step into the walled fortress immediately sense the presence of otherworldly beings, but it is the melancholy Lady Marion de Bruer whose spirit is most often encountered around the grounds. After all, those who have committed the ultimate crime of murder often cannot find peace in death. Lady Marion is a perfect example of this. For she raised her hand not only against the man she had given her heart to, but against herself as well. The fact that her actions were justified seems not to have appeased her conscience, because Lady Marion still walks the earth centuries after her death.

Lady Marion resided in Ludlow Castle under the protection of the lord of the manor. In those days, castles were almost completely self-sufficient and home to every class of people, from the lowliest servant to the most pampered royalty. Had fate not intervened, Lady Marion's destiny would have been to live out her life in Ludlow Castle, but she fell under the spell of a charismatic knight, Sir Arnold de Lys. Their romance developed into a fatal attraction.

Sir Arnold loved Marion, but he held no allegiance to the lord of Ludlow Castle. In fact, he was a known enemy of Ludlow, and therefore every meeting between the two lovers meant possible death for both. They would not be forgiven for their treachery. Still, the danger was not enough to stop them from seeing each other.

Their clandestine meetings took place in Pendover Tower, on the grounds of Ludlow Castle. Marion would regularly ascend the steep stairs of the tower, and lower a rope from the battlements to the rocky ground at its base. Arnold then shimmied up the wall to spend a few stolen hours with the woman he loved. Marion knew the risks, but she approached her love for Arnold with wild abandon.

For his part, Arnold adored Marion, but he had a different sort of treachery on his mind. Chance had shown him a way into the fortified walls of Ludlow Castle. For a long time he pushed away all thoughts of betraying Marion, but in the end power won over loyalty. Driven by something stronger than himself, he decided to act on his plan. He secretly amassed a small army and one night he arrived at Pendover Tower with a battalion of knights in his wake, and victory on his mind.

Marion watched in disbelief as the man she loved fought for and won Ludlow Castle. He'd used her as a means to further his ambitions, and it destroyed her. Sir Arnold's betrayal wounded Marion, almost as if he had stuck a sword through her aching heart. He begged forgiveness, and Marion gave it—but Lady de Bruer was not a forgiving woman.

That night she lay nestled in Sir Arnold's arms while he sank into a contented slumber. Marion pretended to sleep as she plotted his murder. When Sir Arnold's breathing deepened, she climbed out of bed and reached for his sword. With her hand trembling, she stood above her lover. His body lay still, illuminated by the soft moonlight shining in through the window. She wiped her moist eyes, took a deep breath, leaned over Sir Arnold and pushed the sword into the pale skin below his ear. She drew it across his throat to his other ear, surprised at how easily it moved through his soft skin. The blood from the gaping wound spattered over Marion and she recoiled, horrified by what she'd done. The sword clattered to the floor and Sir Arnold gurgled his dying breath.

Justice had been served, according to the times, but Marion's life had lost all meaning. Lady de Bruer walked slowly to the window and begged for God's forgiveness. She looked back to where her dead lover lay and uttered a final goodbye, then she leapt from Pendover Tower to her death. The next day, her body was found, broken and lifeless on the rocks below.

Marion de Bruer died in the 12th century, but her ghost has never left Ludlow Castle. Visitors have seen it in the vicinity of the Hanging Tower, or it is wandering wretchedly through the grounds of the graveyard. Every year, on the anniversary of the death of the lady and her knight, despondent screams shatter the night. The betrayal that Marion experienced on her last day on earth continues to haunt her in death.

People who have seen Marion's ghost report that a strange sense of desperation settles upon them, making them want to get as far away from her as possible. Some areas of the castle suddenly become icy cold and an invisible presence is often felt near Pendover Tower. In fact, there are so many ghosts that live within the castle that it is not always possible to identify who is who, but it remains one of England's most haunted places.

Armando and Inez
MESILLA, NEW MEXICO

Violence and strife marks the history of New Mexico, so it is not surprising that this sprawling southern state is also a hotbed of ghostly activity. The town of Mesilla lies south of Santa Fe in an area that was known for years as "no man's land" until Mexico seceded it to the United States in the early 1850s.

The area is a historian's gold mine. Strategically located on both the El Camino Real and Butterfield Stagecoach routes, Mesilla played an important role in the settlement of the Wild West. It was here, in April 1881, that Billy the Kid was tried and sentenced to hang for his crimes (he escaped and was later shot dead by Pat Garrett in Fort Sumner).

In the heart of Mesilla is an opulent Victorian-era mansion built by the powerful import-export Maese famly. The building is now known as the Double Eagle Restaurant, named for an 1850s 20-dollar gold coin that is stamped on each side with America's national bird. Now on the National Register of Historic Places, the Double Eagle served as a military hospital during the Civil War, and later as a governor's headquarters.

Armando and Inez are two young lovers who continue to haunt the Carlota Salon, a room in the Double Eagle that was once Armando's bedroom and the scene of their brutal murder over 150 years ago. Ultimately, though, this is not a story of murder, but a story of a love stronger than death.

Armando Maese shouldered all the responsibilities of the eldest son born into an aristocratic 19th-century family. His mother, Señora Carlota Maese, was a proud and haughty woman. She harbored great plans for her son's future, especially that he marry into the upper class of Mexico City, thereby increasing the family's fortunes and prestige.

But Armando fell hopelessly in love with Inez, a servant girl employed by his family. Pictures of Inez show a dark-eyed beauty whose thick ebony hair cascaded to her waist. Although Armando struggled to suppress his feelings for her, eventually he lost the battle and confessed that he loved her.

Soon the teenagers were inseparable and their clandestine meetings and stolen kisses became common knowledge to the household servants, who delighted in the affair. Rumors of their illicit love quickly spread to

Mesilla, but the villagers guarded the secret. Señora Maese's snobbish manners and elitist attitude guaranteed her unpopularity, and the locals disliked her as much as they liked her son.

Armando's mother began to notice changes in her son. His moods swung from giddy to somber and he spent long hours away from home. In spite of his attempts to hide his feelings, his mother noticed that he seemed preoccupied with Inez. She confronted him, aware that young men will develop eyes for servant girls. She didn't mind as long as it was only a casual liaison, but when he confessed the depth of his love, she was furious. That afternoon she fired Inez and forbade her ever to step foot in Double Eagle again. She reminded Armando of his duty to his family, and extracted a promise from him that he would forget Inez.

Armando had no choice but to agree, but he couldn't give up Inez. They began meeting in secret whenever his mother left the house. The thought that Armando might disobey her wishes never crossed Señora Maese's mind, until one day she returned home unexpectedly early. The servants were acting odd, and Armando's mother became suspicious.

"Where is my son?" she demanded, but she was met with a protective silence. She searched the whole house, finally tiptoeing to his bedroom. Behind the door, she heard soft murmuring. Furious, she pushed her way in.

Inez and Armando were entwined in each other's arms. Horrified, Señora Maese stumbled backward out to the patio. How could her son be so disrespectful? How dare he disobey her? Disoriented, she bumped into her sewing table. When she found her balance again, her hand closed around a pair of shears. She picked them up and walked purposefully back to Armando's bedroom. She was in control of her body, but out of her mind. Her movements were zombie-like, her limbs stiff, her face set in a terrible grimace. She held one hand behind her back while the other hung limply at her side. The teenage lovers, still half-dressed, cowered as she approached them. Her cheeks were flushed, her eyes wild.

She stopped inches from Inez, her earlier calmness replaced by a savage fury. She raised her hand and plunged the scissors into the young girl's chest. Not once, not twice but over and over again, until the blood of Inez covered both of them. Armando lunged at his mother, begging her to stop, but she seemed deaf to her son and blind to her actions. He flung himself in front of Inez and felt the hard steal blades plunge into his back.

"No!" he screamed. "Mama, no!"

Señora Maese stopped. She stood paralyzed, the bloodied shears in her trembling hand. At her feet her son struggled to breathe. "No," he repeated. Armando crawled to the dying Inez and took her in his arms for the last time. Tears flowed down his cheeks as his own life seeped out of the ragged stab wound in his back.

"Armando," Señora Maese whispered.

By now the servants had gathered in the doorway. They stood silently as Armando planted a tender kiss on Inez's bloodless lips. As her last breath warmed his mouth, Armando's eyes closed.

"Armando," Señora Maese repeated. She never spoke a single word again for as long as she lived.

Hearing her voice, Armando opened his eyes, but he looked through his mother, gazing instead into a corner of his bedroom. Slowly the shocked expression on his face was replaced by a smile of recognition. Inez was calling him to join her in death. Armando closed his eyes and within three days, he was reunited with his love.

The spirits of Armando and Inez remain in the Carlota Salon. They are playful ghosts, child-like specters who move tables and chairs around the room, throw wine glasses and whisper each other's names into the ears of visitors. Sometimes the heady scent of Inez's perfume fills the salon, and sometimes her image is seen floating through the Double Eagle. She is dressed in the clothes of her time—a long black skirt and a frilly white blouse. Two chairs, rarely used by guests, are worn, the fabric faded by the vague outline of two human bodies. Photos of the two have been taken, and no one who has been there doubts their existence.

The many people who have felt the presence of Armando and Inez describe them as happy ghosts, who found in death what they couldn't have in life. There have also been reports of mysterious poltergeist activity within the restaurant, but investigators are unsure who is responsible for it.

The Dueling Grounds
NEAR WASHINGTON, D.C.

March 22, 1820. Two men stand back to back. Their figures are silhouetted against the long, swaying grasses that move gently in the gray dawn light. Their shoulders are rigid, their faces expressionless. It is impossible to guess what emotions they are feeling. They hand their topcoats to their seconds, who accept them solemnly. Even though the morning is cool, dark patches of moisture stain their pressed white shirts, and if one looks closely one can see the veins on their foreheads and necks throbbing. Neither has slept the night before, each knowing that for one of them there will be no tomorrow. A group of men watch silently in the shadows cast by the trees that surround the dueling grounds. The nervous chatter of the early morning has been replaced by an uncomfortable silence. Some anticipate the gun battle with excitement, but a few, the minority, already lament the certain loss of life. All are lost in private thought.

The seconds have taken care of all the details. The chosen weapons are pistols—large caliber, smoothbore flintlocks, heavy and inaccurate even in the hands of an expert shooter. The paces are ten and the count is three. Negotiating a peaceful settlement has proven useless; neither man will apologize. Although it is early, the hour between light and dark, the duelists and their followers have ridden down the narrow dirt track that leads out of Bladensburg, stopping for a strong drink at the local inn before heading to the dueling grounds. The innkeeper is accepting bets on who the survivor will be. They have crossed the narrow bridge that spans Blood Run Creek. Everything is ready. The men have already shaken hands, have already said goodbye to their loved ones, each with the promise that it will be he and not his sworn enemy who will return home victorious with his honor still intact.

In nearby Washington, D.C., in a stately home across from the White House in Lafayette Square, a woman sits in darkness, her curtains drawn, her small hands clasped together. She struggles to hold back the tears, and refuses to let herself imagine how life will change if her love is taken from her. She thinks she would rather die than face a future without him. And all she can do is wait—for either the familiar sound of his footsteps coming up the path or a knock on the door.

She bows her head and begins to pray. She knows that it is God who chooses which man is right and which man is wrong in a duel. It is God who directs the fatal bullet and protects the innocent. She knows this is true, but still she is terrified. What if God makes a mistake? She apologizes silently to the heavens for her blasphemy and tries to ignore the sick feeling in her stomach.

The men, mortal enemies for years and even more so in these last few minutes, stand tall and straight. There is nothing more to be said. They face each other and wait for the count. The rules dictate that they cannot fire their weapons before the count of one or after the count of three. They draw on one and shoot. The birds rise from the nearby trees, startled, and then the moans of the wounded men fill the air. Both have been hit and fall to the ground, where their blood mingles with the blood of those who

Many jealous rivals squared off at Bladensburg dueling grounds, causing the area to become haunted.

have gone before them. Only Commander Stephen Decatur, naval hero and beloved husband, will die this day. The bullet enters Stephen just below his ribs on his right side. Commodore James Barron, the challenger, is luckier. He is hit in the leg and manages to hobble away from the scene on the arms of his supporters.

Susan Decatur, Stephen's wife, hears the carriage roll up in front of their home. She rushes downstairs, thanking God with every step. Her heart leaps in joy and she rushes to the front door only to find herself staring into the face of her worst nightmare. "No!" she cries. "No! Not Stephen!"

Four men carry her beloved Stephen into the house. One of them is red-eyed and the rest say nothing, but avert their eyes from hers. Stephen's clothes are soaked in blood. The men lay him out on the sofa and smelling salts are pressed to his nose, but he is too weak and too wounded; nothing can save him now. He lingers for three hours in a semi-comatose state until a final, painful death rattle announces his departure from the living. Susan collapses over his body and the men have to drag her away.

In the 1800s, dueling was the method by which honorable men—that is, men of the upper classes—solved disputes. It was an old tradition that had been imported from Europe. The scene above was repeated 50 times with different characters and different outcomes on the Bladensburg dueling grounds. It is small wonder that the ghosts of some of those men still haunt the killing field more than a century and a half after the practice of dueling was finally outlawed in the United States.

In 1838 it was decreed that a gentleman had the right to refuse to fight a duel without fear of mockery or reprisal. In effect, duels became illegal; participants were not allowed to serve in public office and it was considered a criminal offence. The practice was driven underground and eventually it became unfashionable.

But it was too late for many victims of the gladiatorial sport. The names of those men who fought or those who died dueling are a litany of some of America's most recognized names: Daniel Key, John Sherborne, Aaron Burr, Andrew Hamilton, Andrew Jackson, William Carroll, Thomas Hart Benton, John Sevier, Sam Houston, Stephen Decatur—the list goes on.

The animosity between Stephen Decatur and James Barron, the men described above, had grown and festered for many years. Once they had been brothers in arms, but when Barron was accused of cowardice and was court-martialed, Decatur sat on the jury that demanded his five-year expulsion from the navy. Years of correspondence between the two men documented their growing antipathy. Barron challenged Decatur to a duel at the earliest possible time after his return to the United States.

By this time, Stephen and Susan Decatur were members of Washington's tony social set. Their home was a gathering place for the powerful and the wealthy. At 41 years old, Stephen Decatur was entering a comfortable phase of his life with the woman he dearly loved at his side. His death shocked Washington society and devastated his wife. She left their home and died of a broken heart.

Stephen's ghost has been seen at the Bladensburg dueling grounds, but most often he is seen staring out the window of his bedroom in the home he loved in Lafayette Square. Susan's ghost remains with that of her husband. Many witnesses have heard her sad cries as she wanders about her house, mourning her husband.

Other spirits haunt Bladensburg dueling grounds—today unrecognizable except for a marker on Route 450 in Maryland. Daniel Key, a son of Francis Scott Key, composer of "The Star Spangled Banner," died there at the youthful age of 20 after a silly dispute with his friend regarding the speed of a steamboat; he remains earth-bound. General Armistead Mason accepted a challenge to duel from his cousin, Colonel John McCarty, to defend the honor of a woman. Mason died on the grounds and McCarty received a bullet in his hand. It traveled up his right arm and exited at his shoulder. He could no longer use his right arm, nor could he forgive himself for killing a man he admired and was related to. He slowly went insane.

McCarty is another Bladensburg phantom whose confused apparition has been seen wandering near where he shot his cousin. Congressman Johathan Cilley lost his life in a duel with Congressman William Graves, who acted as second and stand-in for a close friend. Graves was an excellent shot, and Cilley didn't have a chance. He died immediately, leaving behind a wife and three children. No wonder his unhappy ghost continues to haunt the place where he died so unexpectedly.

It is still possible to visit the Decatur home, which is now a museum, in Lafayette Square. It is located at 748 Jackson Place NW. Bladensburg is near the Fort Lincoln Cemetery northeast of Washington, D.C., in Prince George County. Look for the historical marker on Route 450 and be prepared to come face to face with the living dead—men from two centuries ago who still have not accepted that they must rest in peace.

The Muller House Haunting
NEW ORLEANS, LOUISIANA

Behind the façade of wrought-iron balconies, cascading flowers, gumbo and jazz, New Orleans harbors a dark underbelly. Also known as "The City of the Dead," it occupies a metaphysical gray zone where the border between the living and the dead is blurred and indecipherable. America's most haunted city is rich in stories of disembodied spirits and unexplained occurrences, but none is so gruesome as the following tale of love and betrayal.

A wandering eye or a jealous heart can destroy lives. Perhaps no two people have had to pay such a high price for human failings as Mr. and Mrs. Hans Muller, a young German couple who immigrated to New Orleans in the 1800s, full of hope for a new life together in the New World. But their hope turned to despair, and they found their lives literally and figuratively ground to a halt when the ties that bound them to each other became like a prisoner's chains.

The Mullers arrived in New Orleans with a strong work ethic, a commitment to each other and a recipe for delectable old-country pork sausages that ensured their success. Soon they had developed a loyal customer base, and they were making an enviable living manufacturing and retailing sausages. People liked shopping at the Mullers' sausage factory. The meat was always delicious and the Mullers knew all their clients by name. Business boomed, and soon they were able to purchase a fine home on Ursulines Street. Mrs. Muller was proud of all that they had achieved, and although the hours of work took a toll on her body, she never complained. Instead, she delighted in the realization of their longstanding dream.

Hans Muller, although he disguised it well, did not share in his wife's happiness. In his eyes, the countless hours of hard labor had turned her old before her time, and as the years waned so did his commitment to her. He found himself embroiled in an unexpected affair with another woman. Before long, Hans found himself too much involved, and the only solution was to rid himself of his wife.

It's likely that Hans tried to shake off the terrible thoughts that began to crowd his waking moments, but in the end passion won over logic. One fateful night, Hans Muller's wife followed the routine that had been hers for what had seemed like a lifetime. She closed the shop, cleaned the counters, emptied the till and began the nightly chore of sweeping the factory floors. When her husband approached her from behind, she probably thought nothing of it, until the cord he clenched in his hands tightened around her neck.

Mrs. Muller was a hefty woman and she fought for her life. Her death was slow and agonizing. Only when she lay lifeless in a heap at his feet did Hans begin to realize the implications of what he had done. The customers loved her, and she would be missed. Besides, there was the problem of disposing of her body.

Panicked, he dragged her across the unswept floor and over to the sausage machine. Within a half-hour, Mrs. Muller was no more. But Hans Muller's problems had just begun. For weeks after her murder, he lied about her whereabouts to inquiring customers and worried friends. At first he said Mrs. Muller was ill, but when people wanted to visit her, he told them that she had gone to see her mother. He had no regrets about his act of hate, only fear of the possible repercussions. His only respite was the freedom he now had to spend with the woman he loved.

He kept his relationship with his lover a secret, but with time rumors began to spread throughout New Orleans about Mrs. Muller's prolonged absence. People noticed that the to-die-for sausages didn't taste the same anymore—they were gritty and sometimes bits of fabric were mixed in with the meat. Hans Muller's appearance had deteriorated. He'd lost weight, stopped shaving and seemed exhausted and nervous.

The sausage-maker had begun to fold under the pressure of the constant inquiries about his wife. To make matters worse, he'd run out of excuses, his lover had begun to tire of him and his workload had doubled. One night he'd just finished sweeping the shop floor when he heard the deep rumbling of the sausage machine. Puzzled, he went to investigate. What he saw has become legend in New Orleans. He came face-to-face with his dead wife hoisting herself out of the sausage machine, her face a raw, unrecognizable mess, her body streaked in blood. She reached her mutilated arms out toward him and began to moan. Mr. Muller recoiled in horror, then raced screaming into the street where his neighbors had gathered. Pulling himself together, he explained to them that he'd woken from a terrible nightmare, that he was overtired and he thanked them for their concern. Had it all ended there, Mr. Muller might have got away with murder, but his dead wife had different ideas. She returned to him every night until everyone who knew him began to suspect him of killing her. Still, there was no proof.

As the days passed, the discovery of proof became less likely, until one day an unsuspecting customer bit down on Mrs. Muller's wedding ring. This symbol of eternal love became the object that proved Mr. Muller's betrayal. When the police burst into the sausage factory, Mr. Muller had already begun his penance. They found him huddled in a corner, screaming that his wife was coming to get him. Too crazed for prison, he was locked up in an insane asylum, but even there he could not escape the vengeful ghost of his wife, who haunted him until he took his own life.

The people who bought the sausage factory from Hans Muller saw Mrs. Muller's ghost on many occasions until her husband committed suicide. The factory has been torn down, but Mrs. Muller's ghost continues to haunt the rooms of the home at 725 Ursulines Street. Not surprisingly, the former Muller residence has become a popular attraction on New Orleans ghost tours.

We can only hope that one day Mrs. Muller's ghost finds peace, but for now she remains earthbound, trapped in the drama that ended her life.

The Angry Soldier
WEST VIRGINIA

Many strange things happened during the bloody years of World War I. Men died in horrific circumstances that remain incomprehensible to this day. In West Virginia, for instance, a man lay dying on his living room floor. Thousands of miles away, far across the ocean, at exactly the same time, his killer lay dying in a muddy trench somewhere in Europe. There is only one explanation for this scene, and it is a paranormal one. Read the story and then decide what you think.

Two brothers lived in the same house high on a hill in a small town in West Virginia. They both secretly loved the same girl. She was a wealthy young woman who was wary of fortune hunters and who had been raised to choose her future husband with care. Although she liked both young men, she thought the younger brother was more sincere, so when he proposed to her she accepted. Before they could marry, however, he was called up to fight in the war with Germany. He left secure in the knowledge that his older brother would keep a protective eye on his fiancée until he returned from the overseas, or until his brother joined him on the battlefield. But the older brother did not keep his word. Instead he began to court the girl, eventually persuading her to marry him. Theirs was not a happy marriage, and the girl soon realized she should have waited for her fiancé to return home.

On Christmas, he did just that. He arrived unannounced, and was furious to discover his brother's betrayal.

How did a soldier return to America and murder his deceitful brother if he himself had been killed in World War I a week before?

A shouting match quickly ensued between the two men, which ended when the older brother told the soldier that he would shoot him dead if he ever returned to his home.

Much later that night, under the light of the full moon, the younger brother did return, armed and angry. He marched into the house, withdrew his revolver and shot his brother through the heart. Then he fled. The wounded man died shortly after, but not before he told the whole story to his wife. She called the police, who gave up after an exhaustive search for the killer.

The following morning, on Christmas Day, a telegram arrived at the home of the older brother. His widow opened it with shaking fingers, and read and reread the impossible words, which began: "We regret to inform you that…." Her brother-in-law had been killed in action the week before.

Love Gone Astray
CASTLE CSEJTHE, HUNGARY

The almost surreal beauty of the Countess Erzsebet Bathory hid a woman so barbaric that the Hungarian government ordered the records of her crimes sealed and her name banned from mention for a century following her death. Nevertheless, if one travels today into north-western Hungary, one still senses the unhappy spirits of more than 600 girls that "the Blood Countess" brutalized and butchered in the torture chambers of the dungeons of Castle Csejthe. But while Erzsebet's bloody history remains a blemish on Transylvania's past almost 500 years later, the story of Hungary's "National Monster" is little known in North America, although it was the Blood Countess who inspired Bram Stoker to write *Dracula*.

Erzsebet was born in Nyribathor, Hungary, in 1560 to a powerful family that included members of the royal family as well as some of Hungary's most influential political figures. After years of inbreeding, the family had been tainted with both physical and mental defects, but these characteristics were common to European aristocracy and were tolerated.

Erzsebet was a spoiled child, disliked by her caregivers and subject to violent epileptic seizures. At an early age, her cruel nature became apparent in the obsessive enjoyment she derived from torturing small animals. Yet the young Erzsebet was extremely bright. In a time when even the most privileged males could neither read nor write in their mother tongue, Erzsebet was fluent in both spoken and written Hungarian, German and Latin by the time she was 11 years old.

As a young girl, Erzsebet saw many peasants die—discipline for disobedient servants was both swift and fatal, especially since their lives were of little or no value. Some historians and criminologists, in attempts to explain her aberrant behavior, have claimed that her upbringing was largely responsible for her actions. What is certain that her cruel and sadistic nature had formed in her early years.

On May 5, 1575, at the age of 15, Erzsebet entered into an arranged marriage with Count Fernencz Nadasky, a 26-year-old warrior whose brutality on the battlefield had earned him the name "the Black Hero of Hungary." The marriage meant the union of two influential families. Nearly 5000 guests attended and Erzsebet's wedding presents were substantial. She received a castle called Csejthe as well as the 17 villages that surrounded it, and her husband adopted her surname so they could exploit the power that went with it.

It was a marriage made in heaven—or hell, depending on how you look at it. Although the count spent most of his time fighting battles, he returned home often enough to teach his young wife the intricacies of sado-masochism.

This painting of the Hungarian proto-vampire Erzsebet Bathory offers little indication of her twisted lust for immortality.

Erzsebet proved a willing student. By the time she was in her early 20s she, with the help of her childhood nanny, engaged in the systematic torture of servant girls on a regular basis. And regardless of how severe the abuse got, nobody could have stopped her. She was the law.

For Erzsebet, life was almost perfect except that her hated mother-in-law lived with her at Csejthe, and she was bored a lot of the time. There were no children in their marriage until Erzsebet reached her mid-20s, when her first daughter arrived in 1585. Over a ten-year period the couple had three more children.

In retrospect, it is unlikely that those children shared the same father. Erzsebet overcame her isolation and boredom in the arms of the young men who populated her villages. For a brief period, she ran away with a dark-haired peasant named Ladislav Bende, but returned when she tired of him. Her husband was not pleased when he found out about the affair, but he forgave her.

Perhaps Erzsebet's story might have ended here, had not a handful of equally warped people entered her life. The first of these was her aunt, Countess Klara Bathory, and two noblewomen were soon engaging in sado-masochistic orgies. The second was her servant, Thorko, who trained her in witchcraft and introduced her to Dravula and Dorottya, two witches deeply involved in the occult. Erzsebet became a witch, and she delighted in live sacrifices of large animals such as horses and cows.

Count Fernencz returned home less and less often, and in 1600, the 51-year-old count was killed while away at war. Erzsebet, now in her early 40s, became obsessed with aging. As she began to fear for her own mortality, her cruelty towards others increased exponentially. She threw her mother-in-law out of her castle and was afterward free to do exactly as she pleased.

She discovered what it was that really pleased her a short time later. One afternoon she sat in front of her mirror, staring at her image while a young servant girl brushed her long, dark hair. Erzsebet, more consumed by vanity every day, was afraid—as frightened as Snow

White's evil stepmother had been when she asked the fateful question: "Mirror, mirror on the wall, who's the fairest of them all?" The girl was also afraid. She took great care in running the brush smoothly over her mistress' head, the strokes long and even because she lived in terror of the countess. Her efforts were fruitless. When she accidentally pulled a strand of hair, Erzsebet flew into a rage, turning and striking her servant. She hit her so hard that she drew blood, and when she saw the girl's blood on her hand, she paused and then began to rub it slowly into her pale skin. The mirror told her all she needed to know—it was as if the lifeblood from her teenaged servant had rejuvenated her own complexion. She called for Thorko and Dorottya, giving them precise instructions as to what they were to do.

Thorko and Dorottya leaned the girl over a large pail and sliced her throat. She bled to death, and then Erzsbet immersed herself in the pail, enjoying her first blood bath.

The countess, immune from the law by her status in society and doubly protected by the late count's sizeable loans to the government, looked at the 17 villages she owned and saw a hunting ground. From then on, young girls were brought to the castle under the pretense of work and turned into Erzsebet's private fountain of youth. The castle cemetery soon filled with the bodies of her victims. The local minister, at Erzsebet's request, provided legitimate burials for the girls, but as the number of her victims rose into the hundreds, Erzsebet's loyal and terrified servants began to bury the girls in the open fields near the castle grounds. There wasn't a soul who could stop the killing. Erzsebet and her team of torturers carried out

If Csejthe Castle is haunted today, it's probably because of the unspeakable cruelty perpetrated there long ago.

their evil deep in Castle Csejthe's dungeons, and Erzsebet documented every killing.

As the body count grew, so too did the suspicions of the villagers. Erzsebet became more and more careless in the burials as she aged. Believing herself to be completely immune from the law, she extended her hunting grounds to the manor houses that lay within the vicinity of her castle. For a time the authorities turned a blind eye to her actions, until the daughter from a more influential family disappeared. Bowing to the demands of the girl's father, the Emperor of Hungary ordered Count Juraj Thurzo to put an immediate stop to the countess' activities.

Thurzo didn't want to get involved—Erzsebet was actually his cousin—but he was given no choice. On December 31, 1610, he led his army division into the castle. What they saw there repulsed even the most violent among them. The castle was littered with the dead and dying bodies of Erzsebet's young victims.

The soldiers found over 60 bodies in various stages of decay. The discovery of Erzsebet's diaries confirmed what the villagers had known for so long. Filled with the names of her victims, the diaries detailed the gruesome ways in which they had died.

The emperor ordered that the countess be walled into her own torture chamber for the duration of her life. A slit was left in the wall so that she could receive food and water. The Blood Countess survived for four years in her homemade hell. Her guards found her face down on the stone floor, her food untouched, her body rigid in death. She was 54 years old and had terrorized her small fiefdom for nearly 40 years. Today, the memory of her terrible deeds still haunts the land around Castle Csejthe, as do the souls of all the poor girls who died at her hands.

Murder from the Grave

NORTH DAKOTA

Carol and Lorna Mae Eberele lost their mother in a terrible house fire when they were very small. The two girls grew up taking care of their elderly father. The sisters had very little in common and their personalities were very different. Carol, the eldest, was domineering, aggressive and lazy. In spite of her beauty, few people liked her, although she had her father wrapped around her little finger. She ruled the house with an iron hand, and expected to be obeyed no matter how unreasonable her requests were.

By contrast, Lorna Mae was a rather homely but cheerful girl. People described her as being "strong as an ox." She ran the family farm and she did it well. Although not blessed with her sister's stunning good looks, her shining personality and optimism guaranteed that she was well liked within the community.

Next door to the Eberele Farm lived a widower, Ben Berg, and his three young children. For a long time, Ben had his eyes on Lorna Mae to be his future wife, and he waited patiently for her to mature into adulthood. He knew both of the girls well and rightly judged that the younger of the two would make a loving mother for his three children and an invaluable addition around the farm.

Finally Ben proposed, and Lorna Mae accepted immediately. She was surprised and thrilled that he had chosen her rather than her much prettier sister. Carol reacted angrily. She had always assumed that she would one day be Ben Berg's bride, and from that moment on she began to hate her sister. She did not keep her thoughts to herself. She pleaded with Ben to change his mind and marry her, and she demanded that her sister refuse his hand, but for once Lorna Mae held her ground.

For the wedding, Lorna Mae sewed a beautiful white dress, but as the big day approached she began to feel ill. Her father wanted to send for the doctor immediately, but Carol ignored his request until Lorna Mae's pain became so acute that she eventually had to agree to fetch him. She hitched up the wagon and headed for town, but did not return for hours. When she did return, she was alone and claimed that she had been unable to locate the doctor.

By this time, Lorna Mae was writhing in agony, so Carol loaded her ailing sister into the wagon and set off the find the doctor. Once again, she returned home hours later alone. Lorna Mae, she explained to her distraught father, had died of acute appendicitis, but there was a silver lining—now she was free to marry Ben Berg. Unfortunately for her, Ben Berg did not want to marry Carol.

At Lorna Mae's funeral, Carol demanded that Ben marry her in front of all the mourners. She cajoled and wept and threw a tantrum until the poor, grieving man agreed. He placed Lorna Mae's ring on her finger. In front of embarrassed friends and family, Carol then insisted that the wedding dress her sister was to be buried in be removed from her body. "I will need the dress," she stated, "more than she will now."

Carol got her wish. In July 1930, in the sweltering North Dakota heat, she and Ben Berg stood before a preacher, ready to exchange their vows. Because Carol had insisted on a formal outdoor ceremony, the wedding

A wedding dress, generally a symbol of love and beauty, spells death in the story of Carol and Lorna Mae Eberele.

guests were extremely uncomfortable under the burning sun. They wiped their brows with damp handkerchiefs and hoped the service would be a short one.

Ben stood miserably beside his bride. He glanced at her occasionally and saw the temperature was affecting her too. She was not a strong woman to begin with, but now beads of perspiration rolled down her pale face and her lips were drawn back in an unnatural manner. She began to sway on her feet and raised her arms to clutch her neck. As Ben reached out to steady her, she collapsed in his arms. He called for the doctor and lowered her gently to the dry, cracked ground while the wedding guests formed a circle around her still body. The doctor pushed his way to the front and knelt to examine her. No pulse, no heartbeat. Carol Eberele died seconds before she became Mrs. Berg. She was buried beside her sister a few days later, wearing her sister's wedding dress.

The autopsy results stunned the whole county. Carol had not died a natural death, but had died of a massive intake of embalming fluid. She had been poisoned, but by whom? The doctor provided an answer that nobody could accept: Lorna Mae was the guilty party. She had avenged herself from the grave.

The wedding dress that Lorna Mae had created so lovingly for her own nuptials had clothed her for the three days leading to her burial. During that time the embalming fluid had been absorbed by the material. When Carol stole the dress from her sister's body and put it on her own, the poison began its ugly work. As Carol stood out in the noonday sun, her pores opened and the fluids seeped into her skin and killed her.

Lorna Mae had achieved her goal and was able to rest in peace.

3
The Ties
That Bind

The Gray Lady of Penrose
FREMONT COUNTY, COLORADO

East of Penrose in Fremont County, Colorado, are the crumbling ruins of the old Glendale Stagecoach Station. Established in 1861 by John McClure, the station became a favorite stopover for westbound pioneers. The travelers dreamt of better lives or untold fortunes in the gold fields of California and Colorado. Today not much is left of the two-story reddish adobe structure, but Kathleen Cooper remains. She is one of Colorado's most famous Gray Ladies—the name given by paranormal investigators to forlorn female ghosts who have died of broken hearts or unrequited love.

In 1877, Kathleen Cooper and a handful of others lived at the Glendale Station. It would have been a lonely life, except for the myriad of travelers passing through it. Kathleen did not lack for outside company. Perched on the edge of Beaver Creek, the station boasted a beautiful garden where locals and coach passengers alike enjoyed welcomed respites from everyday life.

One spring morning a group of gold prospectors arrived by coach from Santa Fe, New Mexico. Among them was Julian LaSalle, a tall, handsome Virginian who was on his way to Leadville, Colorado. He, like the rest of his fellow passengers, welcomed a 24-hour stop between stages. After a bath and a good meal he found a tranquil spot in the garden to stretch out in the cool grass. Nearby, one of the scouts from the stage line played a sad melody on his harmonica. The music lulled Julian into a meditative mood. He contemplated the opportunities that lay ahead of him and the life he'd left behind. The clear notes of a girl's voice eased him back into the present. Curious, he decided to cut short his nap to investigate the source of the singing.

Kathleen Cooper was also drawn to music—that of the scout. She made her way down to the river's edge garden and began to sing along with his playing. Little did she guess that her impulse to accompany the harmonica would change her life forever. Julian followed her voice, thinking it to be the most beautiful sound he'd ever heard. He fell in love with Kathleen Cooper the second he saw the slender, blonde beauty swaying gently to the notes. Julian approached her and introduced himself. From that moment on, the two were inseparable. Julian decided not to catch the next morning's stage, but to stay in Glendale one more day. He would have stayed forever if it were possible, but he'd promised an old friend that he would help him out with his stake in Leadville, and Julian was a man who kept his promises. The next morning he reluctantly prepared to leave.

Kathleen watched in torment as he boarded the stagecoach. How could she love this man when she'd spent so little time with him? But she trusted her instinct, pushed aside her doubts and called out his name. Julian turned, and they rushed into each other's arms. When they finally parted, they promised to write each other daily, and Kathleen agreed to become Mrs. LaSalle. They set a wedding date for the spring of the next year. The last words Kathleen Cooper said to Julian LaSalle as the coach pulled out of the Glendale Station were, "I'll wait for you. I'll wait here until I am your wife."

Julian and Kathleen corresponded throughout the long winter. They wrote to each other every day. Kathleen awaited the arrival of the mail coach, and then she would take Julian's love letters and sit down by the river to read them over and over again. In them, he often referred to their approaching wedding day. While Julian toiled on his friend's claim in Leadville, Kathleen stitched a beautiful satin wedding dress. Each stitch was created in love. Then, when the leaves reappeared on the trees and the first flowers pushed out of the earth, Kathleen received a letter from Julian. He would be at the Glendale Station in two days. Prepare the wedding ceremony, he wrote her. Two days would seem like two years!

She arose early on the day of his arrival, donned her wedding dress and waited expectantly for the arrival of her lover and soul mate. Her heart fluttered every time she heard approaching horses, and sunk when the rider turned out to be someone other than her groom. As the days wore on with no sign of Julian, her anticipation turned to dread. Kathleen grew increasingly anxious, so her friends and family tried to reassure her. "Minor delays along the road are inevitable," they said. But by dusk she knew in her heart that something had gone terribly wrong.

Darkness fell, and Kathleen became inconsolable. Some of the men mounted their horses to ride out in search of her missing groom. Kathleen retreated to the second-story balcony where she had a better view of the road. Each time she heard the hollow echo of hoofbeats on the road she rushed forward. "Julian," she called, but Julian never appeared. Even so, Kathleen refused to give up her vigil. She'd promised to wait for him, and neither the passing hours nor the pleadings of her friends could make her break her oath. She would wait for him no matter how long it took.

Hours later the posse of men returned to the Glendale Station. They rode in slowly, their bodies hunched low in their saddles, their eyes glued to the dusty trail. Kathleen didn't have to be told—she saw the lifeless body of her fiancé draped over the back of his horse. As impossible and cruel as it seemed, Julian was dead. He had been robbed by highwaymen and brutally murdered.

His distraught bride-to-be remained stoic for the funeral, but as the last shovel-full of red Colorado earth covered Julian's coffin, Kathleen's will to live vanished forever. From that day forth, she refused food and drink and she refused to speak with or listen to anyone. In a last-minute attempt to save her life, her doctor ordered her separated from her memories. He sent her to live with a distant aunt and uncle in Canon City. But they couldn't help her. Nobody could. Kathleen Cooper had made up her mind to die.

By the fall of 1878, her body had wasted away to almost nothing. The outlaws who had stolen Julian's life would soon have the life of Kathleen Cooper on their hands as well. Hardly six months after the death of Julian LaSalle, Kathleen Cooper had willed herself into an early grave. Her wish to join her fiancé had been granted. She died peacefully in her bed in Canon City, but her restless spirit returned to the old Glendale Station.

Paranormal investigators have identified the Glendale Station as a hive of ghostly activity. Many tourists have spotted the gloomy silhouette of Kathleen Cooper. The Gray Lady of Penrose stands in the door of the station, her white satin wedding gown billowing around her ankles, forever waiting for the return of Julian LaSalle.

Anna and Jeroboam
BLOOMFIELD, KENTUCKY

A simple Internet search on "gravestones of Kentucky" brought up the following information about Jeroboam O. Beauchamp: "Convicted Murderer, Figure in the Beauchamp-Sharp Tragedy." Further investigation reveals these faded words on his gravestone:

> *In memory of*
> *Jeroboam O. Beauchamp*
> *Born Sept. 24, 1802,*
> *And Anna, his wife,*
> *Born Feb. 1786*

Jeroboam Beauchamp was born destined for an incredible future. The son of a wealthy man, he was intelligent, friendly and handsome. At the age of 16, he entered law school and immediately earned the respect of Kentucky's Attorney General, Solomon P. Sharpe, who became his mentor and teacher. No one could have guessed that Jeroboam's relatively short affiliation with the flamboyant congressman would lead to an American tragedy that would end in three deaths and inspire Edgar Allan Poe's stage play, *Politan*.

The young Beauchamp would have made a fair-minded and competent lawyer, had not fate intervened before he was called to the bar. A person's standing in society meant nothing to him. In spite of his blue-blooded background, he despised class-based injustice. Beauchamp was a fair man who treated others as he expected to be treated.

Beauchamp's family lived on a rural property near Bloomfield, Kentucky. Between his studies, he often returned home to visit his father and mother. On one of those visits, he learned that a woman named Anna Cooke had recently moved onto the neighboring farm. She was aloof and very beautiful and Jeroboam wondered what dreadful situation could have compelled such a person to withdraw so completely from society. Beauchamp was a curious man. He began making inquiries and soon learned her story.

Anna Cooke had been born and raised on the Tennessee-Kentucky border, near the small town of Bowling Green. She'd had a good upbringing, but her father had squandered the family money. Defeated and destitute, her parents died. Anna was left penniless, her only assets being her vibrant personality and striking physical beauty. Men from both sides of the border courted her, but Anna Cooke had the misfortune to fall under the spell of Solomon Sharpe. Sharpe led her to believe that their futures lay together, and he charmed her into bed on more than one occasion. When Anna discovered that she was pregnant, he stopped seeing her. He denied being the father, and he left her to take care of herself and the unborn child. Anna's reputation was destroyed. In 1820, some months after Sharpe had abandoned her, Anna delivered a stillborn child.

Anna remained insistent that Sharpe admit that he was the father of her illegitimate child, if only to alleviate some of her own shame. He refused. He denied any relationship with her, and claimed that her pregnancy was the result of a fling with an African-American. Rumors of his liaison with Anna were beginning to negatively affect his political career—the only thing he really cared about. To convince his constituents that he was telling the truth, he produced a document swearing he had nothing to do with Anna Cooke and never had.

Even so, the alleged liaison between Anna and Solomon shadowed him throughout his life and damaged his political career. Anna never forgave him. She hated him, and there is no more destructive emotion on earth than hate.

Jeroboam heard her sad story and immediately felt a deep empathy for the woman who lived next door to his family farm. He began to visit her regularly, and a strong friendship developed between them. They talked easily together, without pretension, and soon they became physically attracted to each other as well. Jeroboam refused to acknowledge the disparity of their ages—Anna was 17 years his senior. Ignoring his parents' protests, he allowed himself to fall in love with her. Anna was slightly more reluctant, and refused his offers of marriage more than once. Finally she said yes, but she set an unusual condition on her agreement to become his wife—Jeroboam must swear to kill the man who had almost ruined her life. It was a terrible thing to ask of anyone, especially of a man smitten, but Anna's mind was still consumed with thoughts of revenge.

He agreed, and in doing so sealed his own fate. The couple married in 1824. By this time, Solomon Sharpe had resigned as Attorney General and was soon to become the House Speaker, a prestigious political position. Sharpe had acquired many enemies over his lifetime, but none as dangerous as Jeroboam Beauchamp, who was willing do anything, even kill, for the woman he loved.

Jeroboam challenged Sharpe to a duel, but the wily politician refused to participate. Jeroboam returned to his wife defeated, but she forgave him. Perhaps in her heart she wanted to forgive Sharpe; she didn't mention his name for several months. The couple lived together joyfully, and the influences of the outside world seemed not to touch them. But as much as she tried, Anna could not let go of her hatred for Sharpe. Eventually she began all over again to urge her husband to fulfill his nuptial promise to her. He did, on July 5, 1825, in Sharpe's home in Bowling Green. Solomon P. Sharpe was 38 years old. Jeroboam was in his early 20s. Here is his confession.

> I put on my mask, drew my dagger and proceeded to the door. I knocked three times loud and quick. Colonel Sharpe said: "Who's there?" "Covington," I replied. Quickly Sharp's foot was heard upon the floor. I saw under the door that he approached without a light. I drew my mask over my face, and immediately Colonel Sharpe opened the door. I advanced into the room, and with my left hand I grasped his right wrist. The violence of the grasp

made him spring back; and trying to disengage his wrist he said, "What Covington is this?" I replied, "John A. Covington." "I don't know you," said Colonel Sharpe. "I know John W. Covington." Mrs. Sharpe appeared at the partition door and then disappeared. Seeing her disappear, I said in a persuasive tone of voice, "Come to the light, Colonel, and you will know me," and pulling him by the arm, he came readily to the door. Still holding his wrist with my left hand, I stripped my hat and handkerchief from over my forehead and looked into Sharp's face. He knew me the more readily I imagine, by my long, bushy, curly suit of hair. He sprang back and exclaimed in a tone of horror and despair, "Great God it is him," and as he said that, he fell on his knees. I let go his wrist, and grasped him by the throat, dashing him against the facing of the door, and muttered in his face, "Die you villain." As I said that, I plunged the dagger to his heart.

After the murder, Jeroboam returned home to Anna. She wanted to run from the law, but he assured her that he had covered all his tracks and that he would never be a suspect in the slaying. This proved to be a fatal misjudgment. Both he and Anna were arrested the next day— Anna for conspiracy to commit murder, and her husband for murder in the first degree. The trial was swift, and Jeroboam Orville Beauchamp was found guilty by a jury that rendered its decision in less than an hour. He was sentenced to hang by the neck on July 7, 1826.

The words are no longer legible on Anna and Jeroboam's gravestone in Bloomfield Cemetery.

Anna Beauchamp was devastated. Her husband had killed for her and now he would die for her. On the eve of his date with the gallows, Anna turned her magic on the guards, and after much pleading was granted permission to spend the night with him in his cell on death row. Nobody, perhaps not even Jeroboam, suspected that tucked into her bodice she had hidden two doses of laudanum and a large hunting knife. Laudanum is a derivative of opium, which was used to treat a variety of illnesses from the 17th century on and could be lethal if taken in large amounts.

In the middle of the hot Kentucky night, Anna and Jeroboam swallowed the poison in a double suicide attempt, but the amount was inadequate. Instead of the oblivion of death, they were racked with severe stomach pains and vomiting. Anna had feared this outcome. She withdrew her knife and persuaded her doomed husband to stab himself. He did so, and then she raised the bloodied blade and plunged it into the soft flesh beneath her heart.

Death, even romantic death, is painful and messy. A guard heard the pair screaming and rushed to the cell, where he found the couple dying in each other's arms. He picked up the knife, wet with blood, and called for help. Both were removed to the infirmary, where Jeroboam was kept alive until his state-approved execution.

Anna remained alive by sheer willpower. As dawn broke, the wagon that would carry Jeroboam and his casket rolled up. Too weak to support his own body-weight, he was loaded by the guards onto the death cart then driven to the gallows. As the trapdoors swung open beneath his feet, Anna inhaled her last breath. Three were now dead, and a baby buried and forgotten.

Anna and Jeroboam left no details unresolved. A letter was discovered leaving instructions about their interment. In it, they requested to be buried together in the same casket in the tiny Bloomfield Cemetery. Their final wish was granted—they still lie together, entwined in each other's arms beneath the Kentucky earth.

For many years, the peace and closure that Anna Cooke Beauchamp sought in life eluded her in death. Her ghost is restful now, but for a long time her spirit walked among mortals. Sometimes she would be seen near her shared grave, at other times walking down the road outside the cemetery. People who heard her speak all report the same utterance: "I must return to my good husband's arms." After so much suffering, one can only be relieved that she has done just that.

Visitors to the Beauchamp gravesite will see a newly erected tombstone that stands beside the original one—now so old that the words etched on its granite surface are no longer legible. But the epitaph is important. The verse was penned by the couple just days before their suicide. Here is the beginning:

> *Entomb'd below in one another's arms*
> *The husband and wife repose*
> *Safe from life's never-ending storms*
> *Secure from all their cruel foes.*

Conwy Castle
WALES

The ghost who haunts Conwy Castle in Wales is motivated by sorrow and revenge. Although he is not a happy apparition, his cheerless tale teaches a powerful lesson to those of us wise enough to listen: in life we must forgive our enemies and we must accept that which we cannot change. To do otherwise is to ensure an eternity of suffering, of straddling two worlds, at home in neither.

Conwy Castle is as magnificent a structure today as it was when Edward I built it in the 12th century. Now a UNESCO World Heritage Site, it sits atop the tomb of Llewellyn the Great, the much-adored Welsh leader who lost his life but not his heroic status among his people. The dark and medieval structure, which once symbolized the brute power of England, looms against a wild backdrop of mountains and sea. More of a fortress than a palace, Conwy is one of the many castles constructed by the English to form an "iron ring" around Wales. Edward I succeeded in his goal to instill fear and humiliation into the hearts of his enemies—the castle is surrounded by a massive wall whose sole purpose was to keep the Welsh out and the British in.

The countryside and coastline of North Wales is dotted with many similar fortresses, like giants on a hostile landscape, but none is as awesome as Conwy Castle. There is much to see here for the historical buff or the curious: foreboding dungeons deep in the belly of the castle, eight perfectly symmetrical towers, battlements offering

The haunted Conwy Castle in Wales is a UNESCO World Heritage Site.
Lord Conwy's spirit wanders restlessly in the Lantern Room.

360-degree views and, for ghost hunters, the spirit of a deceased man maddened by grief.

Upon entering Conwy Castle, one is struck by an overwhelming sense of history. It hangs in the still, damp air like a thin veil separating the past from the present, the earthly world from the nether world. Lord Conwy slips back and forth through this portal in a desperate quest to avenge the unexpected death of his adored wife.

Lord Conwy was a powerful man who took his duties as protector and soldier seriously. If he had a weakness, it was the love he shared with Lady Conwy. It made him vulnerable and human.

Shortly before tragedy struck, Lord Conwy set forth to another battleground, but this time he left behind not just his wife, but also their new baby girl. Their goodbyes were all the more painful. Lord Conwy's men would have been surprised to learn that their fearless leader rode out that day with a heavy heart. Most people knew him as aloof and somewhat frightening. Only his wife knew he had a tender and loving side. Lord Conwy swore to her, before he left, that he would return to the castle at the earliest possible time. He extracted an oath from his servants: swearing them to take care of his beloved wife, and threatening them with death or worse should any ill befall her. They took him seriously. They all knew he was a man of his word with a cruel and revengeful streak.

Week after long week, Lady Conwy waited for her husband to return. The servants watched her closely, never letting her out of their sight and catering to her every need. Her baby brought her newfound joy, and alleviated some of her loneliness, but she still felt incomplete without her husband. Every day she prayed for his safe return home. Finally the day of his arrival dawned. Barely able to contain her excitement, and tired of being constantly watched by the servants, she sneaked off to wait for him alone with her child. She made her way up the steep, uneven steps of the lookout tower, gripping her baby to her chest. It was not an easy climb, but when she got to the top and the Welsh countryside spread out before her, it was all worth it. She would watch for her husband from the highest possible point and be the first to see his victorious arrival.

For hours she gazed toward the Welsh mountains, seeing only an empty landscape. Finally, exhausted and sad, she began the long descent to the foot of the tower. Distracted, and encumbered by her child, she made her way carefully down the rough-hewn stone stairs. They were narrow and uneven—difficult to negotiate even with free arms, but more so with a baby. Halfway down, Lady Conwy lost her footing. A small scream that nobody heard escaped her lips as she struggled to regain her balance, but it was impossible. She and her baby tumbled to the bottom of the stairs. That evening the servants searched frantically for their mistress all over the castle. Finally one of them discovered mother and child at the base of the tower—almost every bone in their bodies was shattered, but they still breathed.

Sick with fear, with the oath to protect Lady Conwy foremost on his mind, the servant who had discovered her and her baby summoned the family doctor. When the doctor arrived, he found the mother and child near death in the Lantern Room. He did everything humanly possible to save their lives, but quickly realized that nothing could be done. He summoned the servants and broke the terrible news: Lady Conwy and her baby would not survive the night.

Lord Conwy's arrival was imminent. None of the servants was willing to greet him with the devastating news. His temper was legendary and they feared him more than the devil himself. They begged the doctor to try harder to save the pair, but it was too late—the hand of death already held mother and baby in its vice-like grip.

"If you can't save them, you shall die with them," the servants told the doctor. They pushed him back into the Lantern Room, closed the heavy door and turned the key. The doctor would face Lord Conwy whether he liked it or not. Now there was nothing left to do but to wait for Lord Conwy's return.

When Lord Conwy rode into the keep, the first thing he noticed was that his wife was not there to greet him. Her absence struck a chord of fear into his heart. In the past, she'd always been there to welcome him. He queried the servants, but they refused to meet his eyes or answer his questions. Instead they sent him to the locked room alone. Lord Conwy, sensing something terrible, ran to the Lantern Room, where he discovered the heavy door ajar and his beloved wife and child stone cold dead and unattended. Somehow the doctor had escaped. The castle and surrounding countryside were searched, but he was never seen again.

Mad with grief, Lord Conwy began to piece together the tragedy that had taken Lady Conwy and his baby from him. His anguish turned into a burning hatred for the doctor. Chaos replaced logic in his mind. He vowed revenge and swore that he would kill the doctor, blaming him for the deaths of his family. Unable to withstand the shock of losing his wife and child, hatred overtook his thoughts and he quickly sank into insanity.

Lord Conwy died within months of discovering his dead loved ones. Revenge was his last mortal thought. Often those who pass away with unfinished business do not rest in peace. The ghost of Lord Conwy is a testament to this restlessness. His spirit lingers in the dank Lantern Room, sensed and seen by many since his downward spiral into insanity and death so long ago.

It would be a brave soul who dares to spend a night in the company of the ghost of Conwy Castle. Let us hope that one day Lord Conwy will find forgiveness so he can join his wife and child in a gentler afterlife.

Captain Mary Becker Greene
ALONG THE MISSISSIPPI RIVER

I am silent on the subject of the afterlife because
of necessity. I have friends in both places.
— Mark Twain

There is no dark side to the following ghost story—nothing horrific that will make your hair stand on end or compel you to check under your bed before you go to sleep. Nevertheless, it remains a ghost story, even if the spirit is a happy one who is welcomed by those who have met her over the years.

Mary Becker Greene was the first woman to pilot a steamboat on American waters. Her story is a story of a life well lived, with a peaceful death at the respectable age of 80 and a purposeful haunting by a content ghost.

For 50 years, Captain Mary Becker piloted the *Delta Queen* up and down the slowly moving waters and bayous of the Mississippi River. Her passion for steamboats began in 1890 at the age of 21, when she fell in love with and married Captain Gordon C. Greene, an experienced riverboat pilot. Together they created the highly successful Greeneline Steamship Company.

In the early years of their marriage, Mary and Gordon were inseparable, and as Mary's love for her husband grew, so did her enthusiasm for life on the river. The hours she spent in the wheelhouse by her husband's side were not wasted. She watched and learned and quickly became his unofficial second mate. More than anything, Mary wanted

With the help of her husband, Mary Becker Greene became the first female riverboat pilot in America.

to be a steamboat captain and Gordon supported her. In 1896, with the encouragement of her husband, she earned her captain's license, followed by her master's certificate, and she became the first female riverboat pilot in America.

Although she began her career piloting under the cover of night so that nobody could see that it was a woman at the wheel, Mary eventually became a loved and trusted figure on the Mississippi. Ma Greene, as she came to be affectionately called, was soon a favorite

Mary is said to haunt the Delta Queen, *which operated with a crew of 80 while she was captain.*

among passengers and other riverboat captains. She proved her abilities when she excelled in a 1903 steamship race from Pittsburgh to Cincinnati, coming in ahead of her husband.

The *Delta Queen* was an enormous ship, 60 feet wide and nearly 300 feet long. She had a crew of 80 and could carry up to 180 passengers. Imagine a tiny woman, barely five feet tall, with a huge personality and you've got a good picture of Mary Greene. Capable and opinionated, she enjoyed life immensely. She was a teetotaler and banned any alcoholic beverages on her fleet, but at the same time she loved to dance, listen to music and regale passengers with stories of her life on the Mississippi.

In 1949, in her room on board the *Delta Queen*, Ma Greene died. She was 80 years old. She was posthumously named to the National Maritime Hall of Fame, an honor she would have delighted in. Shortly before her death, she declared "Were I to live over again, I wouldn't miss a day of the life I've enjoyed."

Captain Mary Greene's spirit still lives aboard the ship that was her home for over 50 years. Many present-day passengers have caught glimpses of her in the hallways or on the decks of the *Delta Queen*, identifying the elderly lady dressed in a long skirt by her portrait that hangs in a prominent position on the steamer.

Most of the time, Ma Greene doesn't interfere with the daily running of the steamer. On occasion she has warned the crew of impending disaster, and the first mate claims it was Mary who introduced him to a passenger who became his wife! Sometimes she shows her displeasure. Shortly after her death, a bar was installed on the *Delta Queen*. Seconds after the first drink was mixed, a barge rammed the ship and the bar was destroyed. To the surprise of the crew, the name of the offending barge was the *Captain Mary B!* Ma Greene remained a teetotaler even from the grave.

In a time when women were so restricted in their choice of profession, Captain Mary Greene was blessed to find a husband who was willing to defy the norms of the day and support his wife in her life dream. Sometimes all it takes is one person to believe in another to make the seemingly impossible possible. It was talent and drive that made Captain Mary Greene strive to reach her goal, but it was the love of a good man that assured her success. Theirs is a happy story and perhaps that explains why Captain Mary's haunting leaves people pleased rather than afraid.

To take a cruise on the opulent *Delta Queen* today is to step back into the world of Mark Twain, when the riverboats ruled the Mississippi. The steamer has been fully refurbished and the crew wear period clothing. Tom Greene, the son of Mary and Gordon, purchased the boat that was his childhood home from the Maritime Commission in 1946. He paid $46,250, a bargain since the original price of construction was one million dollars. Passengers who board the *Delta Queen* today for a tour of the Mississippi will be immersed in southern hospitality: they can listen to the ragtime piano players while enjoying Cajun shrimp or Mississippi mud pie. Those who are sensitive to the spiritual world have a good chance of meeting the original pilot of the *Delta Queen*, and those who are not can rest assured that the grand old lady of the Mississippi is watching out for them.

The Ghost of Mr. Myers
LONDON, ENGLAND

Every day, all over the world, men and women fall in and out of love. Most of us accept this condition of being a human; sometimes it is painful and sometimes it is blissful. After the initial pain following a break-up, we somehow manage to successfully regain our equilibrium and find happiness again. But some of us become mired in misery, refusing to allow ourselves another chance at fulfillment. It is often these people who return after death to the place on earth where they once knew joy.

Mr. Myers was this sort of person. It was 1859. He was a wealthy young bachelor, engaged to be married to the woman he loved. In preparation for their future together, he had just taken out a lease on a new home at Fifty Berkeley Square. It was a prestigious address in the heart of London, close to the finest stores. He counted himself fortunate to have secured the lease on the stately house that had once been the long-term residence of British Prime Minister George Canning.

Life was good for Mr. Myers. He held lavish dinner parties in his opulent dining room and he and his fiancée planned a large wedding. Sometimes when all his guests had left and his servants had retired for the evening, he would sit alone in his den and think about how lucky he was. He had money, he had the love of a beautiful woman and he looked forward to a long and happy life at Fifty Berkeley Square.

But something happened that turned this social man into an angry loner. All his dreams were shattered when, shortly before the wedding, his fiancée got cold feet. She announced that she no longer wished to marry him. Offering no reasons, she simply announced her intentions and disappeared from his life forever. Had she met someone else, or had she perhaps simply fallen out of love with Mr. Myers? We will never know what she was thinking, and neither would he. Her rejection devastated Mr. Myers, who retreated into his own protective shell. As the weeks turned into months, he fired all of his staff, excluding one manservant. He refused to see any of his old friends. They eventually gave up on him and disappeared from his life too.

Mr. Myers methodically drove everybody away who cared about him. He retreated to a small, dark attic on the third floor of the home he had once been so proud of. He stopped washing and stopped shaving. Twice a day, his manservant left a meal in his lonely, dank room, but otherwise he had no contact with the outside world. As Mr. Myers' mental and physical health deteriorated, so did the home where he had thrown such grand parties. Cobwebs filled the corners, windows that broke were not repaired, layers of dust settled on the expensive furniture, and moths demolished the Persian carpets. Outside, the bricks blackened, the paint began to weather and the weeds consumed the gardens that had once blossomed with colorful flowers. Rumors began to circulate in the wealthy neighborhood that the house was haunted. Soon people were afraid to walk by Fifty Berkeley Square; they would cross the street and avert their eyes when they passed by. Small children had nightmares about the once-stately home and its heartbroken resident.

Soon it became known as the "most haunted house in Victorian England." In 1873, 14 years after Mr. Myers had moved into Berkeley Square, and many years after he had set foot outside, he was formally charged with not paying his taxes. He ignored the legal requests to appear in court, refusing to leave his home; eventually the case against him was dropped. The authorities cited the fact that his house was haunted as a reason for him not having to pay what he owed in arrears. The gossipmongers continued to build on the legend. They reported hearing terrible screams and eerie sounds emanating from the house and the local newspapers picked up on the story. The house grew more and more derelict.

Mr. Myers eventually died in the small garret at the top of his house. The property remained vacant for many years. It was assumed that his ghost had joined the myriad of other spectral visitors that were said to reside behind its neglected doors. The house changed hands and the new owners refused to comment on the media reports, some of which were incredibly grisly and included accusations of murder. Four people did die at Fifty Berkeley Square: two of fright, one of suicide and one was mysteriously discovered impaled on the iron picket fence that enclosed the property.

This fourth man was a sailor on the HMS *Penelope*. He arrived in London on Christmas Eve, 1887, with his friend, a fellow navy man. After a night of drinking, they set out to find a place to spend the night. They noticed a rental sign on the house at Fifty Berkeley Square, but nobody was there to answer their inquiries. They needed a place to sleep, so they let themselves in and settled into a third-story bedroom. They were awoken in the dead of night by the sound of heavy footsteps on the wooden floor. They rushed to investigate. One of the sailors was able to escape from what he described as a terrible monster that chased them both down the hall. His friend never got out. Instead he flung himself out of an upstairs window, choosing death on the iron fence below over a confrontation with the unidentified apparition.

Eventually it was discovered that a former owner at Fifty Berkeley Square, Mr. Du Pre, had kept his insane brother locked in the attic, the same room that Mr. Myers had occupied for so many years. Perhaps he was responsible for some of the strange shrieks and thuds that many witnesses heard—but that is only a guess.

What is certain is that for some reason, Fifty Berkeley Square was for years a building that attracted darkness, possibly because it was too long the home of an unhappy and heartbroken man who was never able to recover from the blow dealt him by his fiancée. Prior to Mr. Myers' occupancy of Fifty Berkeley Square, there were no reported paranormal phenomena; in fact, previous residents had been very happy there.

During the time of the alleged hauntings, several people, including Lord Thomas Lyttleton, made attempts to spend the night in the old Victorian home. Lord Lyttleton was a neighbor who was sensitive to the paranormal world. He was a fearless man who liked to solve mysteries, and he volunteered to spend a night in the room that Mr. Myers had once occupied. Armed with two shotguns, he told everyone to expect him in the morning. But after midnight he was attacked by an apparition similar to the one that had accosted the two sailors. He emptied his gun into the shape, but it disappeared before his eyes. Lord Lyttleton did not last the night.

Today, Fifty Berkeley Square is occupied by Maggs Brothers Booksellers, a well-known second-hand bookstore. It is well worth a visit, but don't expect to see any ghosts. The paranormal activity seems to have completely abated, and customers and staff members in the store are able to carry on their business uninterrupted by other-worldly beings. Books stay on the shelves, and any poltergeists or evil spirits seem to have vacated the premises. The legacy of sadness and desperation left by Mr. Myers is gone, and perhaps his story will inspire others who have suffered a broken heart to give life and love a second chance.

Casa de La Paz
ST. AUGUSTINE, FLORIDA

In 1915, J. Duncan Puller moved into his newly constructed home in the quaint town of St. Augustine, Florida. He'd chosen the location of his new home carefully and wisely, with entertaining in mind. The airy, spacious rooms offered awesome views of Florida's lush, hot coastline. At night, he and his family enjoyed spectacular sunsets from their large veranda.

J. Duncan Puller was a generous man, kind and well liked by all. He opened his door to friends and acquaintances, welcoming guests into his luxurious home. When he heard that a young couple he knew was to be married, he contacted them immediately with a characteristically charitable offer. They were just starting out in life and did not have a lot of money. Being a hopeless romantic and realizing that they couldn't afford a proper honeymoon, J. Duncan Puller invited them to St. Augustine for a two-week vacation following their wedding. They accepted gratefully. Perhaps had he known that one of the newlyweds would become a permanent resident in his home, he would not have extended his kind invitation so readily.

St. Augustine was a wonderful place for a young couple very much in love. They spent their days exploring the narrow, winding streets of the old town. Sometimes they lunched in the local restaurants, or they packed a picnic and spent a pleasant afternoon eating, sleeping, talking or swimming in the warm, salty water. The two weeks flew by and they both expressed regret at having to leave the Puller home. It had been a blissful start to a happy union.

On the last day of their honeymoon, while the young woman packed their bags and prepared for the journey home, her husband decided to try his hand at fishing in the rich waters of Matanza Bay. This last-minute decision would prove fatal. He awoke at dawn and left the house at sunrise, feeling somewhat torn at the thought of spending a whole day without his wife. Before he departed, he kissed her gently on the lips and whispered in her ear that he would return to her by early evening. "I love you. I'll wait for you," she said, as their bedroom door clicked shut behind him.

She woke up a couple of hours later to the sound of the wind rattling the shutters on her bedroom window. The sky, which had been cloudless and blue for the past two weeks, had turned an ominous black, and the palm trees bent at impossible angles in the howling wind. The young bride rushed downstairs, where the Pullers tried to reassure her that the storm would blow over and that her husband would return safely from his fishing expedition, but none of them really believed it. St. Augustine was under assault. The hurricane season was upon them. Powerful waves crashed onto the beach and soon the streets were running with water.

The new wife did her best not to worry, but her heart was heavy and she was very afraid. To distract herself, she retired to her room where she occupied her time by preparing for their evening departure, even though a sixth sense told her that they would not be leaving that night. By dusk, there was no sign of her husband, or of his small boat. Still, the young woman carried on optimistically, but as darkness blanketed the coast, and there was no sign of the storm letting up, a dreadful fear for her husband's life grew in the pit of her stomach. *He promised he would return, and I promised I would wait,* she told herself. She planted herself at the top of the staircase, surrounded by their luggage, and waited for him. Nothing the Pullers said could convince her to end her lonely vigil.

By midnight, when he had not returned and the storm still raged, it became clear to everyone in the house that the young man was lost at sea. Still, his wife waited for him all through the night, never moving from her perch at the top of the stairs. In the morning, Mrs. Puller took her gently by the arm and led her back to her bedroom. For days she lay in bed and nobody could convince her that her husband was dead. She refused to eat and only drank sips of water when forced. The Pullers were kind to her, but nothing they said or did had any affect on her depression. She had lost her will to live. Her hosts watched horrified as their once-vibrant, happy houseguest wasted away before their eyes. The doctor could do nothing to combat her over-whelming desire to stop living, and she soon died of a broken heart.

That was a long time ago. After the Pullers left their Matanza Bay home, it was converted into suites. Today, it is a popular bed and breakfast aptly named the Casa de la Paz Bayfront Hotel. Although the Puller home has changed hands, and the original residents are long dead, the ghost of the grieving widow has never left. She still waits patiently for the return of her young husband. Hers is a melancholy ghost, a lost soul. She wanders up and down the plush hallways and opulent rooms, often paus-ing at the top of the staircase to gaze mournfully toward the front door. Sometimes she taps gently on the bed-room doors. Guests have heard her sad voice enquiring, "Is it time to leave yet?"

Of course, her time to leave is long past. How long will she wait for her husband, lost at sea so long ago, to return to her? Tragically, she has not realized that as long as she remains earthbound, she will not be reunited with him. One can only hope that one day she will find a way to join him.

Memaloose Island
KLICKITAT COUNTY, WASHINGTON

Since the beginning of time, humans have struggled to unravel the mysteries of death. All the world's major religions address the issue. If there is life after death, then why aren't departed souls able to return permanently to the world of the living? While some souls come back to earth for brief periods of time, or seem to exist in a parallel zone, to our knowledge none actually reenters life and takes up from where he or she left off. Clearly, for most people the trip to the other side is one-way. The mythology of the Natives of the Pacific Northwest offers an explanation for this age-old question.

Midstream in the Columbia Gorge in Washington State sits Memaloose Island. For centuries it has been an ancient tribal burial ground for local Natives. Memaloose loosely translates into English as "Island of the Dead." Here, exposed to the wind and the sun and the rain, Natives from many different tribes deposited their dead on cedar shelves that were exposed to the elements. The island was an ideal place to leave bodies. It is isolated and safe from predators—or it was until the Europeans arrived. When the Bonneville Dam was built in 1938, most of the land was flooded after the remains of 650 men, women and children were moved to other cemeteries along the Columbia. The following story takes place on Memaloose Island, long before the dam was built.

Many years ago, on the banks of the Columbia River, there was a young man and a young woman who were

For hundreds of years, until Europeans arrived in the 19th century, remains of many local Natives were deposited on Memaloose Island.

very much in love. It was assumed that they would create a family together, but the young man became very ill and died. His lover accepted that he had no choice but to pass into the spirit world, but she missed him terribly. Although he had everything he needed in the spirit world, he missed her too and he thought about her constantly.

One night, as the girl lay under her blankets, a disembodied voice spoke to her. "I am a messenger from the Island of the Dead," said the voice. "Your lover lacks for nothing, but he will not be happy without you. He wants you to join him in the land of the dead."

The girl was frightened when she heard the voice, but she told nobody about her nocturnal visitor. She didn't want to go to the Island of the Dead. She wanted her lover to come back to her. The spirit messenger returned three nights in a row, and finally she told her parents. They became very fearful, insisting that she must obey, or the spirits would become very angry and harm the villagers. "We will take you to the Island of the Dead," they said. "You must try not to be afraid."

Reluctantly, the girl did as her parents wished. The three of them set off in a canoe down the Columbia River, arriving at nightfall. As they neared the shore, they heard the echo of drums reverberating off the canyon walls, and in the soft light they saw hundreds of people dancing. As their canoe nudged up to the shore, four spirits met it. They sent her parents away and escorted the girl up to a large house where her true love awaited her. She spotted him across the immense space and her heart leapt. He was even more handsome in death than he had been in life. They fell into each other's arms and danced the night away.

At dawn, the spirits retired—they were nocturnal by nature. The girl fell into a light sleep, her body pressed against that of her lover. She felt happy and content. The sun crept across the island and touched the girl's skin, awaking her. She opened her eyes and found herself cradled in the smooth, ivory arms of a skeleton. All around her were bones and skulls. The spirits who had been so animated the night before stared at her out of empty eye-sockets. The air reeked of death and decay.

She swallowed the scream that rose in her throat, afraid that the slightest noise would wake the dead. Driven by terror, she fled to the shore, where she found a canoe. She jumped into it and headed up the Columbia River, out of the Island of the Dead and back to the land of the living. Her parents were not pleased to see her and in spite of her protests they insisted that she return immediately to Memaloose Island. They were terrified that the spirits would be angry when they discovered that she had run away. She unwillingly did as she was told, and at dusk she re-joined her lover on the island. He was beautiful again, and she loved him again.

Over time, the girl adapted to the rhythms of the spirit world, learning to sleep in the daytime and stay awake at night. Eventually she and her lover conceived. The child was unique—half human and half spirit—a beautiful baby boy everyone loved. The baby's father wanted his own mother to meet her grandchild, and he longed for his baby to grow up in the mortal world. He sent a messenger to his mother, requesting that she come and visit her grandson, and return with him to his village. She agreed. Secretly he planned to follow them back to life, bringing along all the spirits of the island of the dead.

His mother made the journey down the Columbia and arrived at the island at nightfall. Theirs was a happy reunion and there was much singing and dancing. The spirits placed one condition on the grandmother's visit. She was not permitted to look upon her grandson for ten days. After that, she could return with him to her village, where he could grow up as a mortal. She agreed, but her curiosity got the better of her, and one night she crept into where the baby slept and lifted his blanket. The spirits knew immediately what she had done and reacted in anger and retribution. The baby became ill and died. The grandmother was sent off home bearing a terrible message: From that day forth, the dead would never be able to return to the living.

The grandmother went back to her village, her heart heavy. She never saw her son, her daughter-in-law or her grandchild again until her own passing. Today, most of Memaloose Island lies submerged beneath the waters of the Columbia River, and the bodies have been removed. But when Natives pass by the island, they do so in silence, lest they wake the spirits of the dead who still haunt the island.

A Family Affair
CORRALES, NEW MEXICO

Although he was married, the flamboyant, olive-skinned Luis Emberto kept a lover. Unfortunately, so did his gregarious wife Louisa, whose bloodlines stretched back to an old French family. She was the kind of woman who no man could ignore and who brought out the insecurities in many women. They envied her exotic Spanish-French looks and her mysterious style. In fact, Louisa Emberto was just the kind of woman a lovesick man would rather kill than lose.

In 1883 the Embertos found the perfect home—a rambling hacienda outside of Albuquerque, New Mexico. The structure, built in 1801 by the wealthy landowner Diego Montoya, had a high brick wall that separated the lush gardens of the compound from the inhospitable New Mexico wilderness. But not everything was pleasant at the hacienda. In the lawless West of frontier days, the mulberry trees that had provided shade for lovers had also felt the hangman's noose. Inside the home, the blood of the quickly judged, the condemned and the unlucky had been spilled on the same floors where dancers had moved seductively to the beat of salsa bands.

The Embertos and their teenaged son lived an extravagant lifestyle. Every week they hosted lavish parties where the food was plentiful and the sangria flowed. Neighbors and friends regularly flocked to the hacienda to join in the festivities, which often lasted well into the morning hours. Few outsiders would have guessed that beneath the veneer of merriment in the Emberto home, there lay a festering discontent—a discontent that would lead to a tragedy unsurpassed by any other in the region.

Even though Luis kept a mistress of his own, he was insanely jealous of John Miller, a local man and one of the dozens who found Louisa Emberto to be irresistible. There was nothing out of the ordinary in this, but Miller was the only admirer whom Louisa had invited into her bed.

The catalyst for the tragedy came from an unlikely source. The Embertos' son had long listened to his father's complaints about John Miller. One day, Luis confessed to his son that he could no longer stand the presence of the man anywhere near his wife. He swore that he would kill him if he ever laid eyes on him again. Frightened for his mother, the teenager told her of his father's bloody plan. Louisa retaliated by telling her son of the deep-rooted hatred she secretly harbored for his father's mistress. She convinced him that it was the mistress who was at the root of their family's problems. The young Emberto, not immune to his mother's magnetic personality, decided that it was his filial duty to avenge her unhappiness, and in doing so bring his family back together.

On April 30, 1898, all the characters were gathered at the hacienda. It was a hot spring day and the sun beat down on the desert. Inside the hacienda, Luis' mistress had sought out the cool shade of the courtyard. She settled herself under a mulberry tree and fanned the still air. It was there that the young Emberto spotted her—the woman who he thought was responsible for all his mother's pain. He crept up behind, drew his pistol and fired on her defenseless body. He was a good shot and the bullet met its mark. She died instantly, probably never knowing the identity of her killer. Luis heard the shot and rushed to the courtyard, where he found his son standing over the bloody corpse of his lover. Louisa arrived seconds later and watched in horror as her husband, who carried a gun, and her son began to fire their weapons on each other. Luis saw Louisa out of the corner of his eye. Enraged by what his son had done and convinced that he had been set up by his mother, Luis turned his wrath on her. He shot her at point-blank range. She crumbled to the ground and bled to death as the gun battle continued around her.

Luis turned his attention back to his son. He took aim and fired. His son fired back. Within minutes only one person was left alive. Over the bodies of his parents, the son of Luis and Louisa stood, smoking gun in hand, while the realization of what he had done flooded over him. He became the sole survivor of the Emberto family—victim and perpetrator at the same time.

Since that terrible time, the Emberto Hacienda has undergone many changes. It remained a private residence for many years, until it was turned into the Territorial House, an upscale dining room. In 1987, two families, the Jaramillos and the Romeros bought the historic property, and opened a restaurant under a new name, the Rancho de Corrales. Diners can expect incredible traditional and native New Mexican meals but should not be surprised to witness otherworldly entities in both the bar and dining room.

The long-deceased Embertos have not left their family home, perhaps because their bodies are interred within the walls of the compound, just to the west of what is now the restaurant. The church refused to bury their bodies because of the circumstances in which they died.

In the evenings, while guests enjoy their meals, the ghosts of Luis and Louisa return to their home. They seem completely unaware of the earthly activity around them. It is as if they are still living their lives in a parallel time zone, oblivious to the mortals in the restaurant. The ghosts move chairs about the rooms. They blow out lit candles or light unlit ones. Luckily, they have never tried to hurt anyone. If you are dining at the Rancho de Corrales and notice unoccupied rocking chairs moving rhythmically, you can believe your eyes; it is just Luis and Louisa relaxing after a day of haunting.

The Gray Man
PAWLEY'S ISLAND, SOUTH CAROLINA

So prevalent are sightings of the Gray Man of Pawley's Island that the story was featured on the popular television program *Unsolved Mysteries*. The tale involves a spirit whose quest to be reunited with his true love was never fulfilled. Not to be deterred and in spite of this huge disappointment, he reached up from his swampy grave to save her and her family.

South Carolina boasts some of the most dramatic coastline in the world, and Pawley's Island sits a stone's throw south of Myrtle Beach. Today it is a resort, but the cool waters of the Atlantic Ocean, which offer relief to sun worshippers, can become violent in a matter of hours. The legendary hurricanes that sweep up the Eastern Seaboard have claimed many lives and destroyed many homes. Unless one has witnessed a hurricane firsthand, it is almost impossible to imagine the devastation it can wreak. The forces of nature are powerful, but sometimes the forces of the supernatural, strengthened by love, are even more so.

Spirits return to the mortal world for various reasons, but perhaps the most moving reason of all is when these compassionate beings reach out from the grave to warn a loved one of imminent disaster. Paranormal investigators do not know how they are able to do this, but there are numerous cases that prove spirits are present.

In the 1920s, Pawley's Island was a haven for rich plantation owners who were willing, then as now, to risk

More than 75 years after his death, the Gray Man still appears off Pawley's Island, ready to warn locals of impending storms.

the occasional wrath of a hurricane for the lush surroundings of an island paradise, thick with exotic vegeta-
tion and stately trees draped in colorful mosses. Only
four miles long and a quarter mile wide, the island is a
tiny gem in the Atlantic.

The Gray Man of Pawley's Island was once a handsome mainland plantation owner who fell in love with the
daughter of another plantation owner. She returned his
love. So strong were their feelings for each other that they

found each moment apart excruciating. When they were together, they discussed their plans for their future. When they were apart they longed for each other. Neither one ever guessed that tragedy lay just around the corner. Because of the young man's own responsibilities on the plantation, they were often away from each other, but he visited her whenever he was able.

One afternoon he and his manservant set off to see his fiancée. Because he was so eager to see her, he decided to ride directly across the island rather than take the slower route around the island. It would prove to be a fatal error of judgment. The quicker route was little traveled and there were no marked trails. The young man led the way, pushing his horse to its limit. Halfway across, they entered an unmapped swamp. He galloped straight into the life-sucking mud of a quicksand pit.

Behind him, his manservant watched in horror as his master and his master's favorite horse disappeared into the hungry earth. He screamed for help, but there was nothing his servant could do. Mud as dense as wet clay filled their body cavities and choked the lives out of them. When it was over, the swamp returned to a still and silent state and all traces of the man and his horse had disappeared. Terrified for his own life, the manservant picked his way slowly toward where the girl waited, burdened with his terrible information.

The girl listened quietly as the servant told her what had happened. She accepted the news of her fiancé's death with enormous difficulty and retired to her room to grieve alone. Two nights later, unable to sleep, she got up and headed for the beach, where many happy memories of long walks with her loved one offered her some small comfort. She spotted a figure in the distance, a figure that closely resembled her dead fiancé. Rubbing her eyes in disbelief, she slowly approached him. The outline of the shape was vague, but she was sure it was he. As she neared, the gray figure vaporized into the night air.

Confused and upset, the girl rushed home where she fell into a fitful sleep, only to be disturbed by a terrible dream so realistic that she immediately awoke her father to tell him. Her father listened with concern as she described the nightmarish storm she had seen in the dream. She spoke of a howling gale, of destroyed crops and damaged mansions, of outbuildings torn from their foundations and tossed into the boiling sea. "I think somebody was trying to tell me that we are in danger," she said.

Her father listened and made a decision. By noon, he and his family and most of their servants were bound for the mainland. That night a powerful hurricane struck in all its fury. The girl and her family were convinced that her fiancé had somehow returned to life to warn them.

Much was lost and many people died that night, but the Gray Man of Pawley's Island saved the lives of the girl he loved and the family he had so longed to join. Since that time, he has appeared to warn residents of every hurricane heading toward the Carolina coast. He appears in an indistinct grayish form, striding through the surf. Those who listen to his silent message survive, while arrogant and cynical people often don't.

When the wild 1983 storm struck the Carolina coast, the Gray Man was there just before it. In that hurricane, all the homes and buildings in Magnolia Beach were destroyed. Prior to Hurricane Hugo's brutal assault in 1989, a man and his wife saw the Gray Man wading through the waves. They immediately left for Charleston. The aftermath of Hugo was devastating to Pawley's Island residents—most homes were reduced to rubble, but the home of the lucky couple that had spotted the Gray Man remained intact.

Messages of love from the grave ought not to be ignored. Often, as in the above story, spirits only appear to warn people of death, crisis or danger in a supernatural attempt to save those who are otherwise destined to die.

The Guardian Angel
ST. HELENS, ENGLAND

Wendy Marsh lives in Vancouver, B.C. I've known her for many years. She leans toward skepticism rather than fancy, which only proves that ghosts choose the families they will haunt, and sometimes even those who don't believe in the spirit world are, when faced with over-whelming evidence, forced to change their minds. Wendy's mother passed the story on to Wendy, and it has now become a part of the Marsh family folklore. Wendy was eager to share it with me, and has no doubt in her mind that it occurred exactly as she told it to me.

Wendy's grandfather, Arnold Holden, seems to have been quite a character. Arnold was one of five sons and three daughters born to a family whose father was a Mersey River pilot. They lived in Liverpool. Wendy describes him this way: "Arnold Holden was a typical young man of his age—15, lively, handsome and bored. He wanted to relieve the boredom by joining any branch of the forces that would have him so that he could join the men fighting in France. This was 1914. Unfortunately, when the war started Arnold was too young to be accepted in the army, so he did the obvious—he ran away from home and lied about his age. He joined up under the name of Arnold Talbot. He won the Military Cross under the assumed name."

Wendy's grandmother, Dorothy Ingham, lived in a tiny village called Peetling Parya, where her father was the local minister. Her father had high expectations that all three of his daughters would marry well, but Dorothy, who was beautiful and strong-willed, intended to marry only for love. And love is what she felt as soon as she met the debonair Arnold Holden while he was on leave. Holden was equally smitten and soon they were married. In Wendy's words, her grandmother was "swept off her feet."

She laughs and continues: "Dorothy's father was educated at Oxford. It must have come as a shock that his daughter would marry as she did but he may have been resigned to it. His daughters had all been rebels. He used to recollect his mortification as he began his sermons, watching his daughters sneak out of the church while the other parishioners stayed to listen.

"After the First World War, Dorothy and Arnold, as was true of many of their generation, believed they had fought the war to end all wars. They became strong advocates for peace. They also lived with a skeptical disrespect for structured British society. My mom Alma describes a life of longing to be 'normal' in a house where parents and grandparents were anything but. Her parents were witty, devil-may-care risk takers.

"The reverend's wife, Elizabeth, was very strange and a bit frightening. According to my mom, Alma, she had what she called a 'gift.'" Wendy pauses and looks at me, and then she begins to speak again.

"In 1937 Dorothy had just given birth to twins in a town called Saint Helen's. Her daughter Alma—my mom—was a young teenager at the time and was caring for Dorothy as best she could. The birth had not been easy. One twin had died and the other remained in hospital, in very grave condition. Dorothy had been sent home but she was also seriously ill.

"Alma went to the door to answer a knock. It was her grandmother Elizabeth. She said, 'Your mother's ill. Take me to her.' Alma was never able to figure out how her grandmother got there, or how she had heard. Alma did as she was told, and then watched as her grandmother 'took the pain' from her mom. Her grandmother sat and rocked, obviously in great pain, and for the first time since she had come home, Dorothy slept and was able to get better."

Dorothy survived. Arnold Holden was eternally grateful to his mother-in-law Elizabeth for preserving the life of his soul mate and partner. Elizabeth has long since passed on. Although she has not made any earthly appearances, Wendy is sure that if she were ever needed, she would be there for her family—a spiritual protector for her whole clan.

The Maiden of Deception Pass
PUGET SOUND, WASHINGTON

The house post rises out of the earth at the foot of Rosario Beach—a symbolic rendering of an age-old legend, carved into an ancient red cedar. The wood is gray and weather-worn from years of exposure to the sun, the rain and the wind. On one side, the one that looks inward toward the land, the carved figure, a female in a plain dress, holds a salmon high above her head. Her opposite side looks out to sea and here her dress is adorned with tiny starfish, mussels and clams—representative of her legendary story. Her hair, in her human form, is long and black and has been transformed into kelp that cascades down her back. She too raises a salmon to the sky. The post was carved in 1983 to honor this mythological creature. She is the guardian of the body of water known as Deception Pass.

Many people, when they think about Deception Pass in Puget Sound, are reminded of Captain George Vancouver's 1792 exploration of the Pacific Northwest. He named the narrow tidal gorge "Deception" because it proved false his theory that it opened into a harbor. Instead, it was a passage between two land bodies. Today only skilled sailors attempt to navigate the churning channel where the sea boils beneath their boats and crashes against the steep canyon walls of Whidbey and Fidalgo Islands.

What Captain Vancouver probably didn't realize, and what few of us are aware of, was that this gorge lay within the ancestral home of the Coast Salish Nation. Although the Salish were not deceived by the geography of the

Deception Pass, so named by the Pacific Northwest explorer George Vancouver, has long been sacred to the Coast Salish people.

coast, their deception by the Europeans was great indeed, perhaps showing how aptly the area is named.

The male members of the Coast Salish were exquisite carvers, who, like many of their neighbors, applied their technical carving skills to the creation of symbolic art forms—in particular the building of house posts and grave posts. These posts told of their rich history, of their mythology and of their beliefs. Today, visitors who arrive on the shores of the Coast Salish village in Deception Pass by land or by sea are met by the imposing 23-foot story pole that communicates the legend of Ko-Kwal-alwoot, or the Maiden of Deception Pass. Even now, people look to her for safe passage. Hers is a story of an unlikely marriage that led to a respected position in the spirit world.

Many years ago, there lived a beautiful young girl whose coal black hair reached her waist and whose personality captivated all who knew her—human and nonhuman alike. She was as comfortable in the sea as she was on land. The raging waters of Deception Pass were her playground and her retreat. She delighted rather than feared swimming through the strong currents. She valued the time she spent with the creatures that lived on the shoreline and in the water, and she always felt protected and safe.

One spring day she dug for clams, as was her custom. She waded into the green water, enjoying the soft touch of the salty air on her smooth skin and the cool sea on her bare ankles. In her palm, she held a clam. Much to her amazement, it leapt from her hand to the water, causing her to laugh out loud, because everybody knows that clams can't jump. It floated just in front of her, so she moved forward and scooped it out of the sea. Seconds later, it shot out of her hand again, landing in deeper water. It was as if it was trying to lead her somewhere, but she dismissed that as ridiculous. She retrieved it again, but it leapt away again and again until the water was up to her neck, and she decided not to pursue it any longer.

As she made her way back to the beach, she felt a strong hand take her own, and a sensuous voice spoke to her. The male voice told her that he had been watching her play at the seashore for a many years. It said it had loved her from afar and would always love her. "You are the most beautiful woman in the world," the voice said.

To this day, the Coast Salish seek guidance through the dangerous waters from Ko-Kwal-alwoot, the Maiden of Deception Pass.

"Please do not be afraid of me." The girl didn't know what to think. She listened but did not reply. Instead she swam to the shore, where she let the sun dry her wet skin. She could not rid her mind of the magical touch of the mysterious hand that had held her own, or the deep resonance of the voice that had spoken to her. She became curious. Who was this creature of the sea?

And so she returned the next day and every day after that. Soon she learned the identity of her admirer, and his intentions. He was the sea. The sea had fallen in love with her, and she with him. Over time, she learned many secrets about the world below the surface, and when the sea asked her to marry him, she readily agreed.

Her father forbade the union. He feared his daughter might die in the strange undersea world, and the thought that he might never see her again broke his heart. But the sea was determined and he told her father, "If you don't give your daughter to me, there will be no more food from my kingdom and your men will no longer be safe in the tidal narrows."

The father ignored the threat, and from that day forth the nets of the fishermen came up empty, the shoreline was devoid of shellfish and every canoe that entered the pass capsized. The Coast Salish people grew more and more hungry and they were afraid that they would not survive. Finally the daughter begged her father to allow the marriage, if only to save her village. He agreed reluctantly, but only on the condition that he could speak with the sea first.

The meeting between the girl's father and the sea was a success. The father gave his daughter to the sea. He asked only two things: first, that the sea would put his daughter's happiness ahead of everything else; and second, that each year she be allowed to return to visit her people. This way he would know that she was safe and happy. The sea agreed, and the couple was rejoined immediately. The whole village gathered on the beach to watch the young girl as she walked into the ocean to be with her new husband. They waited until the waters closed over her head. Now she belonged to the aquatic world and that world accepted her as one of its own. The last thing the villagers saw was her silky black hair moving gently below the surface of the water. She would not reappear until the spring salmon ran again.

The sea was generous, and the people ate well. They were granted safe passage through the narrows and their children played in the sea without fear of drowning.

When the spring salmon were running, she returned as promised. She was thrilled to see her father and reassured him that she was content and that the sea was good to her. But next year the villagers began to notice subtle changes in her. The year after that they saw that she found the air difficult to breathe. The following year her hair had turned to kelp. At last her father realized that her yearly return to land might kill her—she had become one of the ocean people. Because he was sure that she was happy, he released her from her yearly visits.

She never returned, but many have spotted her rising out of the narrows. She watches the passing boat traffic protectively. Sometimes boaters will glance into the swirling water and catch a glimpse of her waist-length hair moving with the tides just below the surface. First Nations paddlers know that if they conjure the spirit of the Maiden of Deception Pass, their boats will move easily through the narrows. They are grateful to her when their nets are full and when their men return home safely.

The pole that sits on Rosario Beach tells her story in rich detail and is a reminder to all the mariners that the Maiden of Deception Pass is guiding them to a safe harbor.

Clover Adams
WASHINGTON, D.C.

Every December over a two-week period, Clover Adams, wife of Henry Adams, visits her old home in Lafayette Square in Washington, D.C. On the same site today is the upscale Hays-Adams Hotel, located in one of Washington's most haunted city blocks. This haunted reputation is partly why the annual appearance of Clover's ghost, dead now for more than 100 years, is considered less strange than it might be elsewhere. Especially when you consider that the young woman died by suicide on December 6, 1885, and it is not uncommon for suicides to return to the places where they took their lives.

While their mansion was under construction, Clover and her husband Henry Adams rented the fourth-floor rooms in the building next door. They were both excited about the house that would soon be ready for them to live in. Clover, who was a brilliant woman, hoped to attract some of America's greatest minds to her salon parties. She knew that if she could keep her dark moods under control, she could look forward to many happy years. She adored Henry—that had never been the problem. But as much as they were able to love each other, neither of them was able to love themselves.

Henry was a prominent Harvard professor, an esteemed writer and a grandson of John Quincy Adams, sixth president of the United States. Marion Hooper, nicknamed Clover by her adoring father, came from a large family that was left motherless when she was only five years old. She loved her father, perhaps too much, because she felt the loss of her mother deeply. After her marriage to Henry Adams, she wrote to him every week about her life in Washington. Her letters were long and full of vivid descriptions of life in the nation's capital. Her father always replied to her well-crafted letters immediately, begging for more correspondence.

Henry and Clover seemed to live a charmed life, though they were childless. Clover was the center of the literary salon life in the nation's capital. She was described once by her husband as "a perfect Voltaire in petticoats." She was also an accomplished photographer in her own right. Their 13-year marriage was a happy one, clouded only by Clover's occasional spells of depression. The philosopher in Henry Adams accepted his wife's dark moods and did not love her any the less for them. On the contrary, he accepted her for what she was and gave her the freedom to explore her interests in a manner highly atypical of women of the era.

The Adams' decision to build a mansion in Lafayette Square in the early 1880s coincided with the death of Clover's father. She was devastated. Mired in grief, and suddenly no longer able to compose the weekly letters to the man she'd depended on since early childhood, Clover began to retreat into herself. She spent more and more time in her rented fourth-floor rooms, sitting on her rocking chair in front of the fire, lost in her own thoughts. Henry Adams, a compassionate man by all accounts, and accustomed to his wife's strange ways, allowed her the solitude she seemed to crave. He continued with his work and oversaw the construction of their new home next door, saying little to friends and acquaintances about the shroud of darkness that had enveloped Clover. Still, he worried about her constantly. He had never seen her so low.

One afternoon Henry came home and found Clover's lifeless body, slumped in her favorite chair in front of the fire. He tried to revive her, until he saw the empty bottle of potassium cyanide at her feet. He knew then it was hopeless. His beloved wife was gone. She'd swallowed a lethal dose of the fluid she used to develop her photos. She left no note—or if she did, Henry never told anyone. He was determined to protect his wife's privacy. Perhaps it was his stoic silence that caused ugly rumors to circulate in Washington. People began to suspect that Henry had murdered his wife. Without proof, no charges were ever laid, but Henry was broken hearted by the rumors. He had loved her more than himself.

Henry made no effort to cleanse his tarnished reputation. He had loved Clover for 13 years, and that love had been returned. He owed nothing to sharp-tongued Washington society. Henry never spoke of his wife again. Even his autobiography made no mention of Clover—it was as if she had never existed. Some saw that as an admission of guilt, or at the very least indifference.

But Henry Adams missed his wife terribly, and her ghostly returns to their rented home in Lafayette Square are proof that she missed him too. Sometimes depression leads people to do terrible things to themselves and to their loved ones. Clover's suicide hurt Henry deeply, but his loyalty to his brilliant wife ensured that for as long as he lived, her name would never be tarnished. Possibly

Henry Adams commissioned this striking gravesite memorial for his wife, whose spirit still returns to her former home.

that is the greatest tribute a man can offer to the woman he adored.

Clover Adams is buried in Rock Creek Cemetery. Two years after her death, Henry commissioned Augustus Saint-Gauden to create a grave marker that would express "the acceptance and intellectually inevitable." The resulting six-foot bronze statue—a haunting form of a shrouded, faceless figure—is considered one of the most beautiful pieces of artwork in America.

When their mansion was completed, Henry moved into it alone. He lived the rest of his life without a partner. In 1918, at the age of 80, he died of natural causes and his body was laid to rest beside Clover's. Their home, and the house next door that they had rented and lived in as a couple, were torn down in 1927, and the Hays-Adams Hotel built on the site. Clover always makes her yearly visit. Staff at the hotel describe her ghost as harmless. Every year, near the anniversary of her death, she returns to the fourth floor, where she took her own life. Sometimes her moods are light and she delights in silly pranks. Alarm clocks go on and off unexpectedly, locked doors open and shut and radios play. At other times, her mood is heavy and dark. She weeps softly or begs startled chambermaids to tell her, "What do you want?" Sometimes her spirit will call people by name or hug them gently. If you visit the Hays-Adams Hotel in the month of December, do not be surprised if you meet the presence of Clover Adams, a women blessed with intellect who could not overcome the death of her father.

4
Lovelorn

Flora Somerton
SAN FRANCISCO, CALIFORNIA

In 1926, the body of a woman was discovered in a sleazy hotel room in Butte, Montana. Nobody knew who she was and the authorities had little to go on. They guessed her to be in her late 60s. Her hands belied a life of labor, probably as a housekeeper or a maid, and she wore no jewelry. Strangely, though, she was wearing an exquisite tulle ball gown with a Parisian label. The gown had yellowed with age, and it had a musty odor as if it had been in a box or suitcase for years. It was estimated to be at least half a century old.

For a long time, the body remained unclaimed and nameless. The local authorities in Montana refused to let the case drop. They pored over missing persons reports from all across the United States, trying to match the body with a name. Eventually their persistence paid off, and their Jane Doe was identified as Flora Somerton. She had been born 1858 in San Francisco. Her family had reported her missing 50 years ago. Her story had been in all the newspapers at the time of her disappearance. Up until 1906, there had been a $250,000 reward offered by her parents for any information leading to her discovery. Her parents had been brokenhearted at the loss of their daughter. When her father died, her mother lost all hope of finding her child. She withdrew the reward money and passed away soon after—a sad and lonely woman who believed that her daughter had predeceased her.

Flora Somerton had been born into a wealthy West Coast family. She grew up in prestigious Nob Hill in San Francisco. She, like other privileged young women, looked forward to her debutante ball—it was to be the high point of her first 18 years, a formal acknowledgment of her arrival in high society and an opportunity to meet young men already approved by her parents. The object, of course, was matrimony.

When the night of the ball arrived, Flora could barely contain her excitement. She, like most of her friends, had anticipated this special night for years, and she was sure that her ball gown was the most beautiful dress in the whole world. She spent all afternoon getting ready. If she noticed that her mother was a little reticent, or her father a little distant, then she didn't say anything. In truth, both her father and her mother were a little nervous about the evening's planned events. There was something that they had not yet told Flora. It would be impossible to put it off any longer. Tonight Flora would meet the man who her father had chosen to be her husband. Mrs. Somerton wished that it did not have to be this way, but she had no choice but to obey her husband. She knew instinctively that Flora would not be happy with the person her father had picked. No young girl could be. Sometimes the world was an unfair place. Men made the decisions and women accepted them. Where was the justice in that?

Before they were to leave for the ball, Flora's parents called her down to the sitting room. There they broke the terrible news to her. Flora was devastated when she heard the name of the man she would be forced to marry. He was old—much older than she—and ugly and boring.

She had imagined herself falling in love with a handsome, smart man closer to her own age. She knew that her life was ruined. Suddenly all that she dreamed of had turned into an inescapable nightmare. In her mind, she had only one option. Flora stuffed her prized dress into a suitcase and fled San Francisco for the rolling hills and open prairie of Montana.

Her parents never saw her again. She never returned to the city by sea. What happened to her between the night of her debutante ball in San Francisco and her death in Butte, Montana, 50 years later remains a mystery.

Flora's childhood on California Street, between Powell Street and Jones Street in the heart of Nob Hill, had been a happy one. Up until she turned 18, when her father tried to take control of her adult life, she had known little strife. Perhaps that is why, when she died, her spirit returned to San Francisco. Neighbors began to see the elusive figure of a young girl skipping up and down the street in front of the Somerton home. She wore a beautiful white ball gown and there was an ethereal nature to her movements.

Sightings of the Nob Hill Ghost, as Flora is fondly called, are frequent even today. If you want to see her whimsical specter gliding up and down the sidewalk, then be sure to visit California Street in the early mornings or late afternoons—these are her preferred haunting times. Flora's ghost is not a shy entity. Sometimes she walks right through the curious, and at other times she passes them silently, leaving a sense of the 19th century hanging in the air. She is friendly and has never shown any desire to frighten or hurt anyone who has seen her.

Warren and Virginia Randall
GRAND RAPIDS, MICHIGAN

Warren and Virginia Randall left Detroit for a new life in Grand Rapids, Michigan, where Warren had secured a job as a brakeman on the Grand Rapids and Indiana Railroad. The year was 1907, and the new couple looked forward to a comfortable future. They'd only been married a short time and were in the "honeymoon stage" of their relationship when they moved into the Judd-White House, an opulent mansion that had fallen into disrepair. For years the home had served as a boarding house, but the Randalls had grand plans to restore the magnificent home to its original beauty. It would be a huge job and costly, but they were young and energetic.

Fate intervened in the guise of bad luck and misfortune. The job of a brakeman, especially in those days, was a dangerous one and accidents were often, if not fatal, debilitating. One night Warren became involved in a terrible rail accident. His leg was completely crushed. In order to save his life, the doctors amputated his limb. They fitted him with an artificial wooden leg that was uncomfortable to wear and difficult to manipulate. Warren lost his job. He slid into a blinding depression, refused to socialize with any of his old friends and began to take out his irrational frustrations on Virginia. Virginia didn't care that the railroad no longer employed Warren. She was just thankful that he was alive, but that didn't seem to be good enough for him. Suddenly their future together was in jeopardy.

The gentle creature Virginia had married became a monster overnight. He distrusted everyone, and as he withdrew into his own world he convinced himself that Virginia was having affairs with every willing man within a ten-mile radius. His paranoid delusions worsened as each day passed. In the beginning he only made her life miserable by throwing false accusations at her at every moment, but as his self-pity deepened, his abuse became more and more exaggerated. When the abuse became physical, Virginia began to seriously fear for her life. Still she remembered the kinder man she had married and was loath to go the authorities and lay a formal complaint. Even so, the police became regular visitors in their home— a result of the frantic calls of frightened neighbors who had been awoken by their appalling arguments and fights.

Late one night, Virginia finally decided that she had had enough. She packed a bag and fled the house. Warren, in spite of his medical condition, stumbled down the dark streets in pursuit of her, brandishing a straight razor and vowing to kill her. The police stopped the chase and once again begged Virginia to press charges, but she refused. Several months later, a broken and terrified Virginia left Warren, telling friends that she believed that she had no choice. If she didn't, he would kill her eventually.

Warren appeared to accept her departure stoically, but deep down his anger seethed and festered. His love for Virginia had long ago turned into a sick obsession. Two years after she had left him, after much cajoling, he convinced her to go for an evening ride with him in his carriage. The Randalls were alone on that ride, so nobody knows what really happened, or what words passed between them as they rolled through the streets of Grand Rapids. Somehow Virginia ended up with Warren back at her old home, the Judd-White House. She would never leave it again.

Once they were inside, a fight ensued. Warren pulled off his wooden leg and attacked Virginia. He beat her into unconsciousness and then he slit her throat with his straight razor. But he wanted more than her life; he wanted to spend eternity with her. Methodically he gathered all the sheets and towels in the house and rolled them up against the doors and windows to ensure the house was airtight. Then he sealed himself and his dead wife in before he opened the gas lines and eventually succumbed.

For two whole weeks, the Randalls' disappearance remained a mystery. They didn't have a lot of friends in Grand Rapids, so nobody put much effort into looking for them. Eventually the stench of leaking gas, mixed with that of rotting flesh, drew the attention of the office clerks who worked in the building next door to the Judd-White House. The gas workers were called. None of them was prepared for the grisly sight that awaited them when they broke into the mansion. The first thing they saw were the unrecognizable remains of Warren and Virginia. The police were only able to identify them by Warren's leg, stained in Virginia's blood.

The Judd-White House remained standing for another 14 years, although no one ever lived in it again. Even street people avoided its dark presence, not because it was unsafe, but because the ghosts of the Randalls remained within its damp walls. Theirs were not quiet spirits.

People reported screams and moans and heard Virginia pleading with her killer to stop hurting her. Strange, inexplicable lights glowed in the night, but the empty thud of Warren's wooden leg across bare floors was the most frightening phenomenon.

The dilapidated house was condemned in 1924, but not even the bulldozers and the construction of a new building could quiet Warren and Virginia. The Michigan Bell Telephone Company bought the land and located its head offices there. Once the telephone workers had been relocated to the new site, strange incidents began to occur. People were afraid to go to work. The Randalls had returned. Telephone subscribers around Grand Rapids started to receive eerie late-night phone calls that to this day cannot be explained. Although several paranormal investigators have found no solid evidence of Warren and Virginia, the people who have witnessed their strange haunting swear that their despondent souls exist in the circuits and switches of Michigan Bell Telephone Company.

"I'll Dance on Your Grave"
BUCKSPORT, MAINE

When I came across this story, both the witchcraft and the indisputable physical evidence intrigued me. During the 17th century, the Salem witch-hunts were in full swing, and echoes of those turbulent times reverberated throughout the neighboring regions for many years after. The facts of the tale of Colonel Jonathan Buck might vary from storyteller to storyteller, but it is familiar to most people of Maine. Is it an urban legend or a haunting ghost story, based on a horrific truth? Read the following with an open mind, and then decide.

The town of Bucksport, Maine, was named post-humously after its founding father, Colonel Jonathan Buck. Married with six children, Colonel Buck personi-fied the word discipline. He was a stern and intolerant man, who was both widely respected and feared by all who knew him. For many years he served as the Justice of the Peace, and as such, he wielded a lot of power within the community. Not all his decisions were fair ones, and some of them were based on superstition and prejudice. One would come back to haunt him beyond the grave. His death on March 18, 1795, represented the end of an era, but his memory did not fade, especially for the large family that he had started.

Fifty-seven years after he passed away, his children's children still remembered him with awe. He had been buried in a plot in Bucksport's cemetery with only a simple plaque to mark his final resting place. His grandchildren thought it would be appropriate to honor his memory by erecting a large gravestone over his burial plot. They did so and were pleased with their efforts to honor their grandfather. Strangely though, within a year of the installation of the new tombstone, the outline of the lower leg of a woman appeared on the thick slab of stone. It was an odd reddish color similar to that of blood. Nobody could understand where it had come from, but the grandchildren were angry and upset that somebody had vandalized their grandfather's grave. Much effort was made to remove the blemish. They tried to scrub it off, but the stain would not come out. They had stonemasons attempt to sand it and to buff it, but to no avail; the shape of the female leg remained engraved in the stone. Finally, after many failed attempts, the stone was replaced—not once, but three times. Each time, the image reappeared. In exasperation Colonel Buck's heirs decided to leave it be. Today his grave attracts many visitors, sightseers and paranormal investigators alike, each group driven by a need to discover the truth.

What is the truth? There are several different versions of this story, but all concur on one thing: the shapely leg is not there by accident. Rather it is the manifestation of a historic curse, uttered from the lips of a woman condemned to death by the colonel. Even the name of the woman, an accused witch, is disputed. Was she Ida Black or was she Comfort Ainsworth? Was she an old hag or a young beauty? Had she given birth to Colonel Buck's illegitimate child, or had she only shared her body with him? Did she die by hanging or in the hot flames of a funeral pyre? And did her leg roll out of the fire to lie in a smoldering heap at the colonel's feet, as some say?

It is impossible, so many years later, to learn the true circumstances of the woman's execution, but what is certain is that she had been embroiled in an affair with the colony's most important official. When he tired of her, an easy solution presented itself: Colonel Buck accused her of being a witch and condemned her to death. He acted as accuser, judge and jury. Three hundred years ago, that wasn't such a difficult thing for a man in his position to do. In neighboring Massachusetts, accused witches had been burned, lynched, drowned or stoned on a regular basis—and these acts didn't evoke the same horror that they do today.

Colonel Buck's falsely accused witch accepted her fate neither easily nor gracefully. As her life slipped out of body she placed a curse upon the head of the man who had betrayed her so cruelly. The words she spoke shadowed the colonel for the rest of his long life and into the hereafter. Here are her words, as reported in "The Witch's Curse Fulfilled," *Sun-Up Magazine*, January 7, 1929:

> Jonathan Buck, listen to these words, the last my tongue shall utter. In the spirit of the only true and living God I speak to you. You will soon die. Over your grave they will erect a stone that all may know where the bones of the mighty Jonathan Buck are crumbling to dust. But listen, all ye people and may your descendants ever know the truth. Upon that stone will appear the imprint of my foot, and for all time long after your accursed race has perished from the earth the people will come from afar to view the fulfillment and they

will say: "There lies the man who murdered a woman." Remember well, Jonathan Buck. Remember well!

Colonel Jonathan Buck lived to be 77—a long time in mortal years, but perhaps only the blink of an eye in the netherworld. The foot first appeared on the anniversary of the accused witch's death, in the year that Colonel Buck was interred.

Although skeptics often mention the inconsistencies surrounding this tale, many become believers when they find themselves standing in front of the grave of Colonel Jonathan Buck. Nonparanormal explanations about the mark on the slab are suddenly no longer credible. A tangible life force emanates from the shapely female leg. Most visitors are reluctant to reach out and run their fingers around the blood red outline etched in the gray stone.

A witch's curse or the revenge of a woman who died unjustly? A tourist attraction or a paranormal mystery? Whoever the woman was, her anger at Colonel Bucksport has not subsided. I think that this is her way of reminding us of the terrible injustice she suffered in the hands of Bucksport's founding father. Helpless to fight him in life, she haunts his final resting place from the grave.

Mary Gallagher
MONTRÉAL, QUÉBEC

On Friday, June 26, 1879, Mary Gallagher and Susan Kennedy made their way down to Bonsecours Market, where they procured two bottles of cheap whiskey and drank away the harsh reality of their lives as ladies of the night in Griffintown, Montréal's notorious Irish neighborhood. Mary didn't know it, but this afternoon was to be her last. Death lay just around the corner, and Susan Kennedy, her friend and colleague, was to be its messenger. Mary Gallagher, invisible in life, was about to become a legend in death.

Michael Flanagan had spent the night in a hotel near Bonsecours Market with Mary Gallagher. He awoke the next morning, hung over, to an empty bed, and decided he'd like to spend some more time with Mary. He quickly caught up with her and her friend in the market, sharing their whiskey and partying away the day. The afternoon was a blur, but Michael enjoyed the attentions of the two women, and when they suggested they continue drinking at Susan Kennedy's home, he readily agreed.

The three of them staggered to nearby 242 Williams Street, where Susan lived with her husband Jacob, and continued on their drunken binge. As evening settled on Griffintown, Michael Flanagan could drink no more. He passed out, dead drunk, while Mary and Susan attempted to polish off the rest of another bottle. That Flanagan slept through the next few hours without sensing any

Montréal's Griffintown, once a working-class slum, remains haunted by Mary Gallagher, who was brutally murdered there in 1879.

disturbance attests to how much alcohol he must have consumed that day.

Mary and Susan had known each other for quite a while. Though they appeared to be friends, Susan Kennedy harbored an intense jealousy for Mary, a jealousy that was about to spin out of control and change the course of both of their lives.

Somehow the conversation turned to men. They began to argue, and then Susan decked her friend, leaving Mary unconscious on the living room floor. Had she stopped there, we would never have known the story of Mary Gallagher, but Susan had only just begun. Spotting an axe propped up against the wood-burning stove, she grabbed it and then began blindly hacking at Mary's defenseless body. In a bloody frenzy, she swung the blade until she severed Mary's head from her torso. She then picked it up and deposited it in a bucket of water near the stove.

When news of the brutal killing spread through Griffintown, residents from all over rushed to the scene of the murder. They wanted to see exactly where Mary Gallagher had been decapitated.

Susan Kennedy's arrest was immediate, and her sentence was harsh. She was sentenced to hang on December 5, 1879, less than six months after she had killed her colleague. There were inconsistencies in the trial, and Prime Minister John A. Macdonald commuted her sentence. Susan Kennedy, prostitute turned murderess, would spend 16 years in a Montréal jail.

Griffintown no longer exists today. In its place is the Carling O'Keefe Brewery. But every seven years, Mary Gallagher returns to 242 Williams Street to haunt the scene of her murder. She comes back, they say, in search of her head, and until she finds it we can expect to see her apparition on the anniversary of her death.

The Mystery of John Robinson
DELAWARE, OHIO

Who was John Robinson? Hunter? Trapper? Artist? Pirate? Murderer? What was his real name? So many questions and so few answers. His true identity can never be confirmed, but the little that we do know of him establishes one thing—he was always one step ahead of being found out. Years after Robinson was last seen, the victim of his cruelty still haunts the banks of the Scotia River in Ohio—a ghostly reminder of an evil that was done to her long ago.

In 1825, John Robinson arrived in Delaware, Ohio. Although he claimed to be a trapper, the locals were immediately suspicious of him. Trappers were common in the small town, and the people who lived there could easily recognize them by the way they dressed, spoke and behaved. John Robinson did not carry himself like a man of the woods. He was a sullen man who gave little away beyond his name. He carried with him far too much baggage for a trapper, and his knowledge of trapping was limited. He only stayed in town for a few days. As soon as he could, he quickly disappeared up the Scotia River, purportedly to lay his trap lines, but it soon became clear that he was scouting for land. He purchased a large, heavily treed section of land next to the banks of the river, closing the deal with bars of gold. Immediately people began to wonder where he had acquired all his wealth.

The townspeople became even more curious when the stranger began to build a monstrous home that many described as a castle. Robinson remained tight-lipped. He spoke to no one unless it was absolutely necessary. Once again, he paid for everything with bars of gold; even the laborers were paid in this way. As the months went by and the castle was finally completed, wagonloads of luxury goods began to roll through town and along the Scotia River to Robinson's enormous dwelling.

The locals had never seen such a collection of beautiful things. Most lived in small houses and had modest incomes. Robinson's wagons overflowed with the best that money could buy—richly colored Persian carpets, ornate chandeliers, expensive crystal and opulent Parisian furniture. The villagers came to the inescapable conclusion that Robinson had more money than he could ever spend, and the less they knew about him, the more curious they became.

The lucky few tradesmen who were allowed entrance to the castle returned to Delaware with incredible stories of wealth beyond belief. The most intriguing tales involved Robinson's artistic talent. According to these accounts, Robinson was an extraordinary painter who had filled his home with his own brilliant canvases. He was prolific, adding new works of art to his walls until there was little room left. The corners of his rooms were piled with the paintings that he could not fit on the walls. Still, Robinson continued to paint, seemingly compulsively.

The paintings offered some clues about Robinson's identity. One of the canvases depicted him as the captain of a ship that flew the skull and crossbones. The workers were intrigued by the painting and returned to Delaware with news that they had at last discovered who he was. Everyone agreed that the mysterious John Robinson was a man fleeing from justice—an ex-pirate seeking to establish himself in a new, anonymous life with his ill-gotten riches in the wilderness of 19th-century middle America.

Of course, Robinson said nothing to deny or confirm this story. Instead, he continued to live a hermit's life. The villagers wondered at his loneliness. How, they asked themselves, could a man with so much to offer chose to live without love or companionship? Eventually their question was answered in the form of an exotic young woman who seemed to appear from nowhere. She had flowing, long hair the color of coal and luminous, dark eyes. Although no one ever spoke to her, the people watched the beauty from as she wandered slowly along the banks of the Scotia River, her head bent and her eyes to the ground. She seemed sad. They noticed that she, like Robinson, dressed in a manner they were unfamiliar with, and they wondered where she had come from and what her relationship was to Robinson.

To this day, this question has never been answered. Were they in love, or was she just another one of his chattels? Where had she come from and had she come freely, perhaps believing that Robinson loved her? Or had he somehow tricked her into living with him in his isolated mansion?

Before the locals were able to find out, she disappeared as suddenly as she had appeared. Often people heard piercing screams ringing out in the dead of the night. Robinson must have locked up the girl in his house! Although they worried about what Robinson might be doing to her, they turned a deaf ear on the young girl's pain for a long time. But every night the screams worsened. Finally, when it became impossible to ignore her tortured cries, a posse of men assembled. They would tell Robinson that her suffering must end, or he risked arrest. They approached the castle in the woods with a mixed sense of dread and anticipation, which turned to disappointment and confusion when they found the house abandoned. There was no sign of life anywhere on the property. Robinson had fled and—stranger yet—he had left behind all of his possessions.

The men wandered through the empty rooms, looking for clues to explain Robinson's abrupt flight. They didn't have to look for long. When unhappy spirits want to be seen, they have ingenious methods to bring attention to themselves. The men were drawn to a life-like portrait of the unknown girl—she was as stunning as they'd always imagined, even more so up close. As they neared the painting they noticed a bloody handprint smeared on the wall below it. The sense of foreboding grew to terror when the face in the portrait began to move and the lips twisted into an attempt at speech.

They didn't wait around to hear what she had to say. They'd ignored her pleas for help in life, and in death they proved to be even more cowardly. Betrayed on both sides of the grave, the ghost of the unknown girl still wanders sadly up and down the banks of the Scotia River. Sometimes she sobs uncontrollably and at other times she is silent, but her screams never fail to instill terror into the hearts of all who hear them.

Even though the Robinson mansion was ransacked and burned to the ground, no trace of Robinson's gold or Robinson was ever found. The location of the girl's body remains a mystery, but her spirit reaching out from the other side refuses to let us forget that a terrible crime was committed against her. This crime becomes even more abhorrent because the people of Delaware did nothing to protect her. Had Robinson, driven mad by loneliness, sent for her believing that he was capable of loving another human being, and then discovered he couldn't? Too often a relationship that develops out of love ends in hate. The romance is short-lived and the consequences deadly. The element of tragedy in this story is especially sad because the unknown girl has not been able to find the peace in death that life cheated her out of.

If you are brave or compassionate enough to confront her ghost, the Robinson Estate is located just north of the Franklin-Delaware county line.

5

A Romantic Miscellany

The Watauga River Bridge
ELIZABETHTON, TENNESSEE

There is a mysterious otherworldly quality that is characteristic to bridges in all around the world. From the Brothers Grimm's haunting fairytales, featuring wicked trolls, to J.R. Tolkien's *Lord of the Rings*, these man-made structures have long figured in literature, folklore and pop culture. They are a link between the natural world and the supernatural world, between the past and the present—an unearthly battleground where good struggles to conquer evil.

In the paranormal world, bridges also act as cosmic magnets for ethereal visitors who have experienced tragedy or premature death in the shadow of these monuments to human ingenuity. Inexplicably driven to return again and again to the scene of disaster, these spirits seem eternally bound to relive the horrific deaths they have either experienced or caused during their lifetimes.

In southern Tennessee, the Watauga River Bridge spans the Watauga River, linking the close-knit community of Elizabethton to Watauga Lake. Constructed in the 1920s, the steel girder bridge instantly became a favorite spot for young lovers hoping to escape the prying eyes of vigilant townspeople and overprotective parents.

Tim Jackson and Wanda Smithson were two such people. In the 1930s the Great Depression was descending on America, but Tim and Wanda were just falling in love. To them, the world remained a magical place full of possibility.

On one evening, not unlike many before, Tim and
Wanda made their way out of the small community of
Stony Creek, near Elizabethton, walking hand in hand
down the moonlit road toward the river. When they
reached the Watauga River Bridge, they were pleased to
find themselves alone. Delighting in their privacy, they
quickly chose a sheltered patch of ground near the
bridge's footings and settled into each other's arms.

Minutes turned into hours, as they always do when
two people are falling in love, and soon the moon hung
high in the sky and Tim realized it was time to take
Wanda home. Perhaps deep in the recesses of his mind,
he already worried that he had kept her out too late.
Reluctantly, but with a long future in their imaginations,
the young couple prepared to leave. After they packed up
their belongings, they climbed up the embankment
toward the road, and it was then that they became aware
of another couple entering their solitude. As they drew
nearer, they realized only one person blocked their
path—a large man whom neither of them recognized.

As they approached him, a glint of steel flashed in his
hand, and before they could react the stranger pulled out
a long knife and plunged it into Wanda's chest. He
stabbed her only once, but the blade pierced her heart and
she was dead before she hit the soft earth. As her warm
blood soaked into the ground, Tim's senses took over. He
heard the sound of a car on the bridge at the same time as
he felt the knife slip under his skin and between his bones.
Bleeding heavily, Tim pushed his assailant away staggered
up to the road, with his murderer only steps behind him.
The car slowed but didn't stop, yet Tim managed to yank

the back door open and throw himself into the lap of the terrified woman riding in the back. Outside the window the driver glimpsed a crazed man brandishing a bloodied knife. He screamed and hit the gas.

At the hospital, Tim managed to tell the police his story. The doctors did everything possible to save his life, but he died only hours after the girl he loved.

The police rushed to the Watauga River Bridge and spent the night searching for Wanda Smithson's body. They found nothing, no trace of blood or personal belongings or anything to reveal the identity of the killer. If it hadn't been for the eyewitness accounts, Tim's story might never have been believed.

To this day, the whereabouts of the remains of Wanda Smithson remain a mystery. Her killer lived out the rest of his days in anonymity, but the ghosts of these three souls, inextricably linked through violent death and passionate love, still hover in the vicinity of Stony Creek and the Watauga River Bridge.

The ghost of the unknown murderer is a malevolent spirit, and people unfortunate enough to have encountered his spirit describe a sense of pure evil enveloping them. He appears at night wearing the robes of a monk, with a hood partially covering the area where his face should be, but there is no face to be seen, only the smooth outline of a skull.

Less threatening, but equally horrific to travelers crossing the Watauga Bridge after dark, are the disembodied sounds of an entity trying to climb into the back seat of the car. When the ghost is successful, it is possible

to hear the door open and close and the thud of someone throwing himself into the seat.

It is best to just keep moving. Sadly these ghosts don't
seem to know how to do that and are stuck in a world of
pain and disbelief. Often an unsolved murder in the physical world leads to a chaotic existence in the spiritual one.
Perhaps a time will come when the ghosts of Tim Jackson
and Wanda Smithson can conquer the evil that lurks
under the Watauga River Bridge and discover the link
between the world of the living and that of the dead.

The Daughters of the Sun
OKEFENOKEE SWAMP, GEORGIA

In Greek mythology, the Sirens were beautiful beings
whose mesmerizing voices promised wisdom, but instead
delivered death to the ill-fated sailors caught in their
melodic net. Few people know that American mythology
also has a mysterious female tribe. In folklore, the
Daughters of the Sun inhabit a utopian island deep in the
heart of Okefenokee Swamp. There is no absolute proof
that Paradise Island exists—no man who has gone in
search of this magical place has ever come back—but
explorers have long been enthralled by the magnetic pull
of disembodied voices in the damp night air.

Those that enter Okefenokee have been warned, yet
when mortal men hear the call of these supernatural
swamp beauties, all previous counsels are forgotten and
they are magnetically drawn to the sources of the magical
songs. Romantically unrealistic notions of endless love

Okefenokee Swamp in Georgia is home to the Daughters of the Sun, mysterious enchantresses not unlike the Sirens of Greek mythology.

replace all logic, and even in the face of possible death, they go, never to be seen again.

The Seminole word Okefenokee translates to "Land of the Trembling Earth"—referring to the 15-foot deep layer of peat moss that cushions America's largest wetland. Situated in the southeast corner of Georgia and extending into Florida, Okefenokee Swamp is an immense ecosystem covering 700 square miles, home to numerous species of wildlife. Alligators and snakes skulk

between the moss-draped cypress trees or lurk ominously beneath the still, dark waters.

Okefenokee also conceals a paranormal world that
reflects its violent history. Indigenous people fled to the
hostile swamp when the white men had destroyed all that
they owned. Tales of murders, thieves and outlaws are
intermingled with the histories of families who lived and
died in the isolation of the swamp.

Many visitors to Okefenokee Swamp have seen more
than they bargained for. There are eyewitness accounts of
UFOs, spherical lights that hover over vehicles, phantom
bears, deer and wildcats, giant warriors, headless ghosts
and ghost slave ships.

The legend of the Daughters of the Sun dates back to
the Spanish conquistadors. Stories of a beautiful, dark-
haired race of women living on an isolated mist-shrouded
island drew the Spaniards to search for Okefenokee, but
with their lives at stake, the Native guides remained tight-
lipped about the location of Paradise Island. The Spanish
gave up, but others followed, and soon the stories of
mystical music and disappearing explorers became etched
in the history of Okefenokee Swamp.

Not everyone described the swamp maidens as kind-
hearted. Some described them as an aggressive, strong
warrior tribe—hunters and predators who would protect
their island and their identities with their lives, if necessary. All described them as incredibly beautiful and
extraordinarily dangerous.

Who are the Daughters of the Sun? Are they ghosts
from the Lost City of Atlantis? Or are they the alienated
souls of Europeans lost at sea? Perhaps they are the woeful

spirits of Native women sent into exile for crimes of adultery. These questions remain unanswered, but as with the Sirens of Greek mythology, their promise of joy turns into an eternity of sorrow. Possibly the message here is that in love, just like in life, if something seems to good to be true, we would be wise to be wary of it.

According to legend, one group of hunters had set out in search of the Daughters of the Sun. They trudged, near exhaustion, over the Land of the Trembling Earth to where they were rescued by these mystical creatures. After they'd recovered, they were set free, but so obsessed were they with the maidens of Paradise Island that they returned—and were never heard from again.

Over 120 canoe routes snake through the myriad islands of Okefenokee Swamp, a National Wildlife Refuge since 1937. Many people who visit the sprawling ecosystem to enjoy its natural beauty have been confronted with its preternatural mystery. One should enter Okefenokee with an open mind, but at the first note of the songs of the Daughters of the Sun, remember to paddle away.

Widow of Washington Heights
NEW YORK, NEW YORK

On a cool September afternoon, in a suburb north of New York City, a group of impatient schoolchildren wait outside the Morris-Jumel Museum for the doors to open. Suddenly, an ethereal figure, clad only in a filmy lavender nightdress, appears on the second-floor balcony and angrily tells the noisy students to "shush." She fixes her large blue eyes on their surprised faces until they are quiet, then, with a barely perceptible nod, she turns and glides *through* the thick panel of the heavy wooden door that leads into her Napoleonic bedchamber.

It takes a long time to calm the children and their teacher down. The museum custodian reassures them over and over again that the ghost is harmless and that they have nothing to fear at all. Finally she is able to convince them to enter the mansion to begin their historical tour.

The ghostly beauty is Eliza Jumel. She has been dead for 100 years but she is still the mistress of the stately Georgian mansion she so loved in life. According to the museum curator, the Morris-Jumel Mansion is home to a host of lost souls, including a talking Parisian grandfather clock that orders visitors out of the house, and two revenge-seeking husbands. Eliza's spirit, however, offers the most intrigue and is the most active.

Death seemed to shadow Eliza since infancy. She was born July 16, 1769. Her young mother did not survive her birth. Lacking both education and money, the teenaged "Betsy Brown" employed her considerable charm and

The haunted Morris-Jumel Mansion in Brooklyn, New York

beauty to exploit the men around her. She managed to claw her way up through the social ranks from poor orphan to prostitute and, eventually, the wealthiest woman in America. She became a favorite of the court of Napoleon I—and a woman who respectable men fought duels over. She was thrice widowed, and according to the angry ghost of her second husband, she was a murderess.

The staff of the Morris-Jumel Museum are enthusiastic about the history of the stately Washington Heights landmark and the ghosts that inhabit it. Roger Morris, a colonel in the British army, built the 8500-square-foot "summer villa" in 1758 for his new wife, the heiress Mary Philipse. Perched at the uppermost point of Harlem Heights, it offered breathtaking and unobstructed views of New York City and the mighty Hudson and East Rivers beyond.

But the Morrises were not destined to enjoy their summer retreat for long. In 1776, war broke out between the British and the Americans. The strategic location of the Morris mansion did not go unnoticed by General George Washington, and the Morrises offered their home to him. It became headquarters for the American Army Command, which quickly lost it to the British. A great deal of violence took place behind its stately walls.

The oldest ghosts, according to eyewitnesses, are revolutionary soldiers, who, like Eliza, seem reluctant to leave the opulent luxury of the hilltop mansion. It is not uncommon for curators and visitors to suddenly find themselves among a group of uniformed men cavorting in the elegant dining room, or to interrupt Eliza entertaining various soldiers in her lavish bedroom. One terrified woman recalls standing in front of a large gilded portrait of a fully decorated revolutionary soldier, when, to her horror, the figure stepped out of the painting and rushed toward her. She suffered only a mild fainting fit, but a less fortunate woman suffered a fatal heart attack after being confronted by a hostile revolutionary ghost.

Following the Revolutionary War, ownership of the mansion reverted back to the Americans, who turned it into a posh inn—Calumet Hall. Once again, the mansion's strategic location, en route from Albany to New York City, shaped its fate. Word spread quickly and the combination of great food and excellent service attracted best of society to the establishment. It became a favorite destination for President George Washington, his family and his cabinet. Men whose names reverberate through history dined in the graceful octagonal dining room—

Many visitors to this mansion have seen a ghostly woman on the second-floor balcony, keeping watch over her former home.

Vice President John Adams, John Quincy Adams, Secretary of War Henry Knox, Thomas Jefferson and Secretary of State Alexander Hamilton, whose love for Eliza Jumel would ultimately lead to his early death.

The death of Eliza's first husband had left her a very rich woman, but moneyed New York rejected her because of her scandalous background. She fled the wagging tongues to Paris. In 1801 she married the wealthy Parisian wine merchant Stephen Jumel. He knew nothing of her past, only that she'd been widowed and that he loved her. With his introductions, she was accepted into the upper crust of European society. Soon, Madame Jumel became a favorite in the court of Napoleon I, dividing her time between Paris and the new home Stephen had recently purchased in New York—the Morris-Jumel Mansion.

But the Jumel marriage was not a happy union. Eliza, in spite of her vast wealth, continued to be shunned by New York society, perhaps because of her numerous extramarital affairs, which she barely tried to conceal. In a tragic love triangle, she drew Vice President Aaron Burr and Alexander Hamilton into a duel at the Bladensburg dueling grounds, which left Hamilton dead and Burr's political career in a shambles.

Monsieur Jumel could no longer ignore the rumors circulating around his wife. Reluctantly he decided to end the marriage. Eliza was devastated, but when Stephen Jumel fell from a carriage to his death, she was she spared the ultimate disgrace of divorce. Widowed and heiress to a huge fortune that suddenly left her the richest woman in America, she did not spend a long time in mourning. Within a year she married 78-year-old Aaron Burr, and a year after that Eliza filed for divorce. Ironically the decree was granted on the day of his death.

Those most familiar with the ghostly presences that haunt the Morris-Jumel Mansion swear that the cheated and jilted Aaron Burr shuffles through the palatial rooms, an old and restless soul intent on revenge.

One of Eliza Jumel's many extramarital affairs drew in former Vice President Aaron Burr.

Eliza Jumel passed away in the mansion at the age of 93. Her caretakers say she'd lost her mind, and that in spite of all her riches, she died a miserable and lonely old woman. Perhaps that is why her ghost still walks the earth, unable to detach itself from the guilt of a dark and shadowy past.

Stephen Jumel's ghost has been more fortunate. His unhappy presence and pitiful moans so disturbed the museum's curator that she finally called in two well-known psychics to try to contact him. After two intense séances, Hans Holzer and Ethel Myers were able to release Stephen's spirit from its earthly confines, but not until he'd made sure that Eliza would not get away with murder.

During the second séance, conducted in the middle of the night, Stephen Jumel told the psychics he died as the result of a pitchfork accident, not a fall from a carriage. The mediums were horrified to hear that Eliza, furious at her husband's request for an immediate divorce, tore off his bandages and watched calmly as he bled to death before her eyes. After this session, Stephen Jumel's ghost, finally avenged, was never seen or heard from again.

Today, the Morris-Jumel Mansion still presides over New York City and its great rivers. The curator in charge of the museum claims that the hauntings continue. Visitors are still confronted by ghostly apparitions, the old grandfather clock still shouts out orders and shakes violently and Eliza Jumel remains the tragic, otherworldly mistress of the haunted house at the top of the hill.

Alone on the Road
RALEIGH, NORTH CAROLINA

On a warm summer night in Jamestown, North Carolina, in 1932, Lydia's mother lay in her bed and stared up at the cracks on her ceiling, tracing each fine line to its end. Her mind careened through the events of the past year. No matter how hard she tried, she could not still her mind or quiet her chaotic thoughts. She longed for the dark oblivion of sleep—sleep that had eluded her for the last agonizing 12 months.

Finally she drifted into the half-world where consciousness and unconsciousness intersect, so that when the knock came to her front door, as she knew it would, she rose with a start. By the light of the moon that streaked through her window, she saw it was two in the morning but somehow she knew that already.

For a second, hope filtered into her being, but she pushed it away, hating herself for allowing its presence in her life at all. She took a deep breath, pulled on her housecoat and padded to the front door, steeling herself for the difficult conversation that she knew lay ahead of her in the next few minutes.

Without bothering to see who it was, she opened the door and fixed her eyes on the man who stood in front of her. He was handsome, with an athletic build, brown curly hair and large eyes so brown they could almost be black. The expression on his face showed concern and worry but also kindness. Even if she'd been capable of feeling fear, she would not have been afraid of him.

Lydia, she thought with a mother's pride, *always went for the good-looking ones.*

The man introduced himself, nervously shifting from foot to foot. "Sorry to wake you up," he said. "My name is Burke Hamilton and I…" His voice trailed off. Lydia's mother was accustomed to this happening. She stopped being angry with these nocturnal visitors months ago.

The woman held his gaze, reaching deep inside of herself to stay calm; she did not want to not cry in front of this stranger, but the tears came anyway. "Excuse me," she said, wiping her eyes. "Please go on."

"I, uh, I picked up your daughter hitchhiking at the Highway 70 overpass. She needed a ride home and directed me to this house. Now I know it must have been your daughter—you two share an uncanny resemblance. You know, she really shouldn't be out there alone," he added as an afterthought.

"How did she seem?" the woman interrupted, because she couldn't help it. "How did she look?"

"Agitated. Scared. Sad. It was strange. She waved me down. She was just standing there in the fog. I might have run her over if I hadn't been paying attention to the road. She gave me her address, and thanked me for helping her out. So I brought her here, but when I got out of the car to open the door for her, she just kind of disappeared. I wanted to make sure she'd got in safely."

The woman sniffled. "I am her mother," she confirmed. "She was wearing a long white dress, wasn't she? She wanted to come home, didn't she?"

Burke nodded. There was so much more he could add, but he felt foolish. The woman in front of him was clearly distressed, and she was acting as if she hadn't seen her own child in a long time. "I was coming home from a party in Raleigh," he said, then decided against offering any more details. After all, it would sound idiotic to say that he had been in a trance-like state when he picked up the girl—there and yet not there at the same time, as if he'd been both the audience and the actor in a play.

The girl had been the same way—ethereal almost— and he had thought he could see right through her when he had glanced at her slight figure in the passenger seat. She sat pressed against the door, somehow terrified of him. "Don't ask me any more questions," she said. "The only thing that matters to me is that I go home, and that you take me there. Thank you."

Then the fog crept inside his car and it was chilly. At just about the same time, he realized that as ridiculous as it might seem, he might actually love this girl. But she seemed out of reach, unattainable, untouchable, unreal— and dark in a sad way he couldn't put his finger on. Her mother was no less strange.

"Her name was Lydia," she said.

Was? Did she say "was"? Burke said nothing and let the silence hang between them. Finally she spoke.

"Thank you, Burke Hamilton. Thank you for trying to bring my baby home, but she can't get here, even though she never stops trying." Her voice shook and suddenly Burke understood that before him stood a mother consumed by grief. At first he had thought she might be on the verge on insanity, but he did not judge her. He did not make judgments until all the facts were in front of him.

Instead he said, "I'm sorry," not knowing quite why.

"Me too," the woman replied, and he thought that if it would help at all, he would wrap her up in his arms and take all her pain away. He stepped forward, but she held up her hand.

"There is nothing more you can do here, except maybe listen to our story and then go away and leave me alone."

So Burke, who was a good, kind man, listened. He forgot about the party he had attended earlier in the evening with his old university friends, he forgot it was almost 2:30 in the morning on a warm night and that he was talking to a stranger on a porch in the little community of Jamestown.

"My daughter, Lydia," she began in a strained voice, "went to a dance in Raleigh last year. She was very excited. I expected her to be home at two, but she never arrived. The policeman arrived instead and he brought with him the worst news a mother can ever hear. Lydia, my only child, had been killed in car accident at the Highway 70 underpass—right about where you would have picked her up."

Burke noticed that although the woman's voice remained steady, her hands shook as she spoke and tears streamed down her face. "If only she could accept her death, then perhaps I could. But Lydia wanders the highway at night. She waves down men, men like you, and pleads for help. They always bring her home, and she always disappears just before she reaches me. It happens all the time. Somehow knowing that she is alone and lost and confused out there is worse even than knowing she is dead."

Burke knew that this was the truth, and that there nothing he could say. He bowed his head and backed slowly down the stairs and into his car. He drove away from Lydia and her mother and their tragic story, but he never forgot them. Some nights he prayed for Lydia's soul to be delivered, but it hasn't happened yet. Lydia's earth-bound ghost is still seen on a regular basis at the Highway 70 underpass. All she wants to do is to go home, but home is in a different dimension now. One day, perhaps, her spirit will realize this.

All the men who have picked her up have experienced the same sense of overwhelming compassion mixed with a feeling of unreality. Lydia seems only to flag down those who are both handsome and kind.

The Ghost of the Georgetown Mansion
SEATTLE, WASHINGTON

Those unfortunate enough to meet a premature and violent death at the hands of another seem to be drawn back to the place and time of their death, like moths to a flame. It seems even more prevalent when the killers are spouses or lovers. Their forlorn victims often find themselves on a nightmarish treadmill on which they eternally reenact the horrific circumstances of their deaths. Although it is frightening for those who witness these phenomena, usually they need not worry for their own safety. Such spirits are usually harmless to all but themselves.

I came across the following story when I was researching ghosts of Washington State. It was first reported by Carol Lind in *Western Gothic* and it immediately sparked my curiosity. Why? Perhaps because the murder victim was an invisible person—a poor young Native woman who remains nameless to this day. Perhaps it was also because the man who so brutally took her life was the man she loved and trusted.

The details of this story are vague, partially because the current owner of the home where the murder occurred has chosen to remain anonymous. The year was 1899, the city was Seattle. The crime took place in a sprawling multi-room house in a section of the city called Georgetown, where brothels and bars flourished. The girl who passed away was one of the many young Native prostitutes who lived and died far away from their childhood homes.

The local newspaper of the day ran a short piece on her death. It was estimated that she was killed at approximately 12:30 A.M. in her bedroom on the second story of the large house. The cause of death was multiple stab wounds. Her enraged killer continued to stab and chop and slash at her body long after she had gurgled her final, tortured breath.

One hundred and twenty-five years later, a Seattle art dealer shook hands with his real estate agent and closed the deal on the house of his dreams. While most home buyers would have thought carefully about a ramshackle old mansion, this man was different. Where others saw ruin, he saw possibility. He planned to make the huge, dilapidated mansion, which was falling apart in the midst of an overgrown garden, beautiful again.

Some of his friends thought he was crazy. Undaunted, he moved into his new home, full of plans for a full restoration. It didn't take him long to realize that he was not the sole occupant of the neglected mansion. His "roommate," however, was not of the living.

Old houses are not silent. The floorboards squeak, the windows rattle, the aged wood shifts constantly on cracked foundations. The new owner anticipated these sounds, and settled in for his first night without worry.

He slept deeply, but only for a short time. In the dead of the night a piercing scream shattered his dreams. He sat up, shocked to hear a disembodied voice screaming the word "No!" over and over again.

A pall of icy air descended on the house. The man pulled the blankets up to his chin in an attempt to warm himself, but the cold was unnatural and inescapable. Above his head was the unmistakable sound of somebody fighting for her life—and losing. Was it a bad dream or were there strangers in his home? Consumed with fear and doubting his senses, he made up his mind to investigate, but the noise stopped as abruptly as it had begun. He began to doubt his own perceptions.

In the half-dream state where relief and fear cancel each other out, he lay down and chose the safety of sleep over the risk of investigation. He had half-convinced himself that what had happened had been nothing more than a bad dream. Still, the first place he went to explore in the morning was the room upstairs from where the disturbing sounds had emanated the night before.

It appeared to be a normal room, no more and no less run down than any of the other rooms in the old mansion. It was empty, which surprised the art dealer—he was sure he'd heard furniture crashing during the fight. Had he imagined the whole thing? He decided that he had, but the next night he experienced the same terrible commotion. Once again, he heard the sounds of a terrible fight, but this time the struggle was followed by the cries and whimpers of a woman. His fear of the night before was replaced by a sense of overwhelming empathy. The noises stopped as abruptly as they had begun. He didn't want to spend another night in the house alone. The next night he invited some of his friends to sleep over. Either he was losing his mind, or he was sharing the house with some otherworldly spirits. Neither option looked promising.

Sure enough, the next night at half past 12 the noise started again and this time there were witnesses. They all heard a quivering female voice pleading, "No, Manny, no," through a torrent of tears.

His friends were skeptical at first. He was known to be a joker and they thought he might be playing a trick on them. When they realized he wasn't, they were spooked. They told him to call the person who had sold him the house and find out if she knew anything. The house agent was initially reluctant to admit any knowledge of the strange phenomena, but with a little encouragement, she admitted that everyone who had lived in the house had heard the ghostly sounds. Beyond that, she knew nothing.

It was the art dealer who discovered the newspaper clipping about the gruesome stabbing that had taken place in the second-floor bedroom. His heart went out to the young prostitute. He did not sell the house as the previous occupants had. Rather, he decided to stay on and complete the restoration. He continued to feel friendly and empathetic toward the young girl, but always in the back of his mind he feared and hated Manny for taking her life.

Perhaps one day the young murder victim will tire of trying to make sense of her senseless death. One can only hope that she will find the peace in the afterlife that she could not find in her mortal life.

The Baron of Featherstone Castle
HALTWHISTLE, ENGLAND

The Baron of Featherstone swirled his wine around in his glass. As he took a long, slow sip and leaned back in his chair, a deep sigh of relief escaped him. The servant hovering at his shoulder replaced the crystal decanter on the heavy hand-carved sideboard. He stepped back discreetly and silently awaited his master's orders. Outside, dusk settled on the River Tyne and shadows played across the granite walls of the castle. A sense of peace, albeit temporary, settled over Featherstone Castle, located on the banks of the South Tyne River near the tiny village of Rowfoot in Northumberland, England. Soon the Great Hall would be filled with the wedding party, but for now both master and servants enjoyed the quiet.

It had been a busy afternoon, but everything had gone off without a hitch. The baron smiled to himself. He felt pleased and rather surprised with his daughter's behavior. She was a strong-willed girl, and he expected more of a fuss from her. She had been subdued and quiet throughout the ceremony, accepting her filial duty with much less protest than he'd expected. At last she'd finally seen the merit in his choice of husband and banished from her memory the totally unsuitable young man she'd been so determined to marry only a short while ago. He gestured for another glass of wine and congratulated himself for a successful end to what could have been a difficult day.

Meanwhile, Lady Abigail, the daughter of the Baron of Featherstone, and the reason for all his worry, tried

On the same day every year, a melancholy wedding party materializes in the woods that surround Featherstone Castle in England.

not to think about the vows she had uttered only a short time ago in the castle chapel. She hadn't meant a word she said. By surrendering to her father's iron will and marrying his wealthy and titled friend, she had betrayed the only man she really loved.

But what choice had she been given? Her lover had let her down. He'd promised he would rescue her from this terrible union, and right up until she'd whispered "I do" in front of all those witnesses, she'd believed in him. The thought of spending the rest of her living days as the wife of her father's choice of groom made her feel trapped and nauseous. How would she get through the wedding night, let alone the rest of her life? She sighed audibly and closed her eyes, trying to pretend that she was anywhere but in a nuptial carriage.

Custom dictated that following the marriage ceremony in the chapel, the wedding party would parade around the perimeter of Featherstone Castle. They would follow the river to the east and then cut through the forest and home. They all set out, except for her father who had chosen to rest for a little while in preparation for the feast to follow. Some of the guests were mounted, some rode in fancy carriages and they all looked forward to the eating and drinking that lay ahead. As the sun sank in the western sky, the party veered away from the Tyne and entered the woods. Music and laughter filled the cool night air. Abigail sat silently beside her new husband, loath to either touch him or to look at him. He seemed oblivious to her foul mood. He was looking forward to sharing a glass with his new father-in-law.

When the baron had emptied his fourth glass of wine, he began to grow concerned. The customary ride around the grounds should not take such a long time. Surely the guests were hungry and thirsty by now. Was it possible that they'd lost their way? Irritated and hungry himself, he sent some of his men out to search. They returned a short time later. Puzzled, they explained that the wedding party seemed to have disappeared into thin air.

The kitchen staff too was becoming restless. The food they had prepared would be ruined, so it was a relief when

Baron Featherstone at last heard the creaking of the drawbridge opening and the muted echoes of horses' hooves on the cobblestones. Finally the bride and groom and their guests had arrived. "It's about time," he muttered to himself. He stood and prepared to meet his guests.

He looked up as Abigail entered the Great Hall on the arm of his new son-in-law. She certainly didn't look or act the part of a happy new bride. The wedding guests trailed behind them, their movements stiff and unnatural. The baron wondered if the newlyweds had perhaps created a scene already. Everybody was eerily quiet, as they filed in one by one and took their seats at the massive dining table. The first thing the baron noticed was the abnormal silence—nobody breathed a word. The group moved in an orderly fashion, each one taking his or her seat around the table. The soft candlelight flickered over their unusually pale skin, and the Baron of Featherstone Castle shivered, suddenly assaulted by a waft of ice-cold air. "Welcome," he called out, but nobody replied.

He stared into his daughter's eyes, searching for a logical explanation, but all he saw was death. She locked her lifeless gaze on him and a tear rolled down her cheek. A thin trickle of blood had coagulated on her hollow cheek. She looked dead—actually they all did, but that was impossible. They were sitting in front of him. The baron looked again. Suddenly he noticed their torn, blood-streaked clothes and frozen faces. A scream of terror rose in his throat, and as he gave way to his fear the ghostly party faded before his eyes. He keeled over in a dead faint.

The baron never recovered, never spoke again and his mind was destroyed. And what of Abigail's lover? What horror did he feel when the ambush he had planned to save the woman he loved resulted in her violent death? To this day, nobody knows. He disappeared, never to be seen or heard from again. But every year at midnight on the anniversary of the wedding, poor, sad Abigail and her wedding party are sighted in and around the woods that surround Featherstone Castle. They approach the draw-bridge, a silent train of ghosts forever reliving a wedding gone terribly wrong.

6
Three's a Crowd

Judge Not

WASHINGTON, D.C.

Still to another
Life is as death;
Home and its idol
Gone with a breath!
Blood on his hands,
Stain on his bed:
Pity them all—
Living and dead!
　　　—C.H. Webb

Under glass in the military wing of the Smithsonian Museum is the shattered lower half of a man's leg. The note below it reads: "Compliments of General DES." General Daniel Edgar Sickles lost his leg at the Battle of Gettysburg in 1863, but he maintained a morbid attachment to his amputated appendage. He visited it regularly, often in the company of the many women he courted throughout his life. In death, the ghost of Daniel Sickles continues to haunt the Smithsonian and is often spotted hovering near the grisly display.

In Lafayette Square, beneath the shadow of the White House, the ghost of Philip Barton Key stares forlornly up at a second-story window in the house that belonged to Daniel Sickles. After a moment, the figure drifts across the square and stops in the exact place where he met his violent death. What bloody ties bind these two 19th-century entities and keep their spirits forever in limbo?

Philip Key and Daniel Sickles lived the privileged lives of men of power. They held impressive pedigrees. Key's father had penned "The Star Spangled Banner" and his uncle held the position of Attorney General of the United States. His close friendship with Sickles, who was assistant to President James Buchanan and an integral part of the corrupt Tammany Hall Democratic organization, ensured his success as a D.C. lawyer. When they met, Key was the widowed father of four children, Sickles the new husband of the beautiful and bright Teresa Bagioli. Sickles and his wife had one child, Laura, suspiciously born only months after their hurried wedding. Fortunately for the congressman and his wife, a bubble of power protected them from the malicious Washington gossip.

Sickles was in his early 30s when he married, and seemed unwilling to give up the habits of bachelorhood. After his wedding, Sickles continued his liaisons with prostitutes. President Buchanan frowned upon his assistant's sexual promiscuity. He had hoped that marriage would quell Sickles' behavior, but it didn't. Teresa was blessed with youth, intelligence and verve, and she suffered from her husband's lack of attention. She turned to the handsome, charismatic Philip Key for companionship, and he enthusiastically complied, easily slipping into the role of loyal friend. His position as a respected lawyer, wealthy widower and Sickles' good friend initially diverted any suspicion around his relationship with Teresa. He accompanied her to socials, ate dinner at the Sickles' home on a regular basis and was considered to be a close and trustworthy friend. Sickles was grateful for the diversion Key offered his wife.

The spirit of Philip Barton Key haunts Lafayette Square, where his affair with a married woman came to a tragic conclusion.

Soon Teresa and Philip were inseparable. They took advantage of Sickles' heavy workload to spend long afternoons behind the locked doors of the Sickles' parlor room. They danced the evenings away at formal balls, but were always careful to maintain an air of decorum in the presence of the congressman. The servants quickly discovered their secret. Fearful of repercussions, Key rented a nearby apartment, also in Lafayette Square. He signaled his availability to Teresa by hanging a string outside the window. Key had many talents and, in his own words, "he only asked 36 hours with any woman to make her do what he pleased."

Washington's gossipmongers might have been able to turn a blind eye to Congressman Sickles' philandering, but they found the behavior of his wife and best friend scandalous. One afternoon, an anonymous letter arrived at Daniel Sickles' office. Reprinted in *Harper's*, it read, in part:

> There is a fellow, I may say, for he is not a gentleman by any means by the name of Philip Barton Key & I believe the district attorney who rents a house…for no purpose than to meet with your wife Mrs. Sickles. He hangs a string out of the window as a signal to her that he is in and leaves the door unfastened, and she walks in and sir I do assure you he has as much use of your wife as you have. With these few hints I leave the rest for you to imagine.

Sickles confronted Teresa with the letter and she denied its contents vehemently. Sickles believed her. A sense of invincibility settled on Philip Key and Teresa Sickles. They became bolder in their affair. Their liaison became common knowledge to all and finally President Buchanan begged Sickles to pay more attention to his wife and less to his work. On the heels of this came another warning—one that couldn't be ignored. The confirmation of the affair meant that Sickles' humiliation quickly turned to rage.

At two o'clock on Sunday, February 27, 1859, under a bright sun in Lafayette Square, Daniel Edgar Sickles advanced on Philip Barton Key. He held two loaded, cocked pistols in his hands. They were aimed at Key's heart. The lawyer was unarmed. He pleaded for his life. A small crowd that had gathered watched mutely, straining to hear Sickles' words, "You must die." Key raised his arms in disbelief, he begged for forgiveness. Sickles emptied the chamber of one of the guns into the body of his old friend. The first bullet wounded Key, the second killed him and the third need never have been fired. There were witnesses. President Buchanan heard the shots from his office. Sickles didn't care. He had his honor to defend. Immediately he turned himself in to the police.

The papers of the day ate up the story. Sickles was painted as a victim, Key as a sexual predator. The congressman's lawyers pleaded temporary insanity and the jury heard all the lurid details of the affair between Philip Key and Teresa Sickles. The congressman forced his grief-stricken wife to write a vivid confession. In it she described exactly what had occurred on those long afternoons in the rented apartment in Lafayette Square. *Harper's Magazine* and the newspapers of the day reprinted her every salacious word. She showed remorse for her behavior. Washington's most influential men, including those in the White House, empathized with Daniel Sickles' humiliation and chose to ignore his own many indiscretions. The courts awarded him with exoneration—he became the first accused prisoner in America to be released under an insanity plea.

Sickles agreed to take back his wanton wife. She died in 1867, a victim of tuberculosis. Her soul rests in peace.

Witnesses carry Key's body away from Lafayette Square in this historical engraving.

Daniel Sickles went on to command position in the Union Army, where he lost his leg at Gettysburg. He was appointed ambassador to Spain and carried on a torrid affair with the deposed Queen Isabella, earning him the name, "The Yankee King of Spain." At the age of 93, he was arrested for stealing $28,000 from the New York State Monuments Commission, but once again escaped sentencing when his friends paid off the missing amount. He died two years later. His soul still walks the Hirshhorn Museum, part of the Smithsonian.

Philip Key knew no justice, although he seeks it for others. His ghost appeared to Secretary of State William Seward to warn him of an assassination attempt in 1865. It also appears regularly outside his former home in Lafayette Square across from the Washington Club, and at the spot where he was gunned down over 100 years ago.

Revenge from the Grave
GRANT TOWN, WEST VIRGINIA

In the early 1930s, in Grant Town, West Virginia, there lived a middle-aged man named Mr. McCaulla. He was a widower whose wife had passed away in childbirth, leaving him the sole caregiver for their six young children. Although Mr. McCaulla held a good position in the nearby mine and was financially secure, he was consumed with loneliness and overwhelmed by his status as a single father. He found it difficult to meet a woman who was willing to become stepmother to so many children, and he had little time for his male friends. He had given up any hope of finding a mate or even a companion when the Domicos, an attractive and hardworking couple, arrived in Grant Town. They'd relocated from nearby Osaga, so that Mr. Domico could find work.

Mr. and Mrs. Domico were much younger than Mr. McCaulla, but they had no friends in Grant Town. They quickly became friends with the lonely single father. The Domicos felt very sympathetic toward the widower and his children. They opened up their hearts to him, welcoming him into their home and treating him like a family member. When the house next door became vacant, they all agreed that Mr. McCaulla should take it. He moved in and settled into a comfortable routine with the young couple. For the first time in years, Mr. McCaulla no longer felt lonely.

Unfortunately, Mr. McCaulla quickly grew dependent on his new neighbors. He began to eat all his meals at their table and spent more time in their house than he did in his own. He was a generous man, and repaid the Domicos for their kindness by showering them with presents and doing handy work around their property. He even went so far as to secure Mr. Domico a job in the mine as a blaster.

On the surface, everything appeared to be fine, but over a period of half a year, Mr. McCaulla grew more and more fond of Mrs. Domico. He made several advances toward her, but she made it very clear that she was in love with her husband and would never consider leaving him for another man. The widower felt rejected and began to resent Mr. Domico. Eventually his love grew into an obsession, and as each day passed he became more and more desperate to have the one thing in life he couldn't—his neighbor's wife.

After dinner every night, when Mr. McCaulla retired to his own house and bed, he would lie awake for hours, unable to stop himself from thinking about Mrs. Domico. He convinced himself that they could have a wonderful life together—if only she didn't have a husband to interfere with his plans. When he could stand it no longer, he decided on a course of action—a course of action that would change everything irrevocably.

One day, when Mr. Domico headed off to the mine, Mr. McCaulla went with him, pretending that he needed to check on his work. He looked over all the charges carefully, before he pronounced them safe. As the men were leaving the mine, he asked Mr. Domico to double-check, just to make sure. Mr. Domico complied and reentered the shaft. Seconds later, an enormous blast shook the mine.

Mr. McCaulla rushed home to break the news of her husband's death to Mrs. Domico. She was devastated, but never suspected that the man who offered her so much comfort and understanding might be the man responsible for her unhappiness. Within two years they were married, and by all reports theirs was a happy union. The children loved their new stepmother, and for the first time in years, Mr. McCaulla knew really happiness.

But that newfound contentment did not last for very long. Within three months of the marriage, Mr. McCaulla's lifeless body was discovered in the mine, in the exact spot where he sabotaged the blast that killed his friend. In his cold hand, a suicide note was found. In it, he confessed to killing his neighbor so that he could be free to marry his wife. His plan had gone awry when the ghost of Mr. Domico began to haunt him. According to the note, the apparition appeared daily at noon and asked the same question over and over again: "Why did you do it? Why did you kill me?"

Mr. McCaulla could stand it no longer and so he took his own life.

Sadly, more lives were shattered in this murderous love triangle. Mrs. McCaulla reacted to her second husband's death with shame and guilt. Unable to cope with her feelings, her mind snapped and she spent the rest of her life in an insane asylum. And what of the six children? Bereft of their mother, their father and their stepmother, they were forced to fend for themselves.

The ghost of Mr. Domico was never heard from again. His earthly revenge on his killer allowed him eternal rest, and he returned to the land of the dead.

The Ladies of Berry Pomeroy Castle

DEVON, ENGLAND

Berry Pomeroy Castle, which is no longer inhabitable, remains one of the most haunted places in England, second only to the Tower of London. The castle was built at the end of the 13th century on land that had been a gift from William the Conqueror to Ralph de Pomeroy—a generous acknowledgment of his loyalty and bravery in battle. Two hundred years later it passed into the hands of the powerful and wealthy Seymour family, in whose possession it remains today.

Like so many Norman castles, Berry Pomeroy has a history of violence and injustice. Although it was partially destroyed in the English Civil War and then gutted by fire years later, it appears that remnants of its tempestuous times survive in the castle's crumbling battlements and dark dungeons. As if by osmosis, Berry Pomeroy Castle retains and reflects the echoes of distant days.

Paranormal investigators, film crews, ghost hunters and many members of the visiting public have witnessed strange phenomena at the castle, accompanied by feelings of fear and sadness when inside the castle. Perhaps it is because the White Lady and the Blue Lady, although separated by time, share a common goal—lust for revenge. Read their stories and decide for yourself why these sorry souls still walk the earth.

Lady Margaret Pomeroy was blessed with a gentle nature and alluring beauty. Such characteristics seem harmless enough, but to Lady Margaret's much plainer sister, Lady Eleanor, they provided reason enough to condemn her sister to a cruel death. Lady Eleanor was ruled by one emotion—jealousy—which she directed solely at her sister.

Lady Margaret Pomeroy had little in common with her sister. She always tried to treat her pleasantly, but even as a small child she sensed Lady Eleanor's barely concealed dislike for her. The one thing they did share was the love of the same man. Which of the two sisters he preferred is not clear; he courted one and then the other, thereby exacerbating an already volatile situation. Lady Eleanor was determined to win his favors at any cost. When the suitor began to lavish his attention upon Lady Margaret, her sister, consumed by jealousy, decided the only way to end the rivalry was to remove her sister permanently.

One night, Eleanor lured her sister to the dungeons beneath the tower that was her namesake. Lady Margaret followed her sister innocently down the long, cold stone staircase into the bowels of their castle. The air was chill and stale, and their lanterns only threw enough light to illuminate the steps in front of them. They rarely went down to the dungeons, and Lady Margaret was curious about what her sister meant to show her there. When they reached the cells, Lady Eleanor stepped aside and convinced her sister to enter before her. Once inside, she slammed the heavy door shut, bolted it and fled. St. Margaret's Tower became Lady Margaret's prison. For days and days the rest of her family searched in vain for her. They combed the woods that encircled the castle, but they never thought to look in the dark subterranean cells.

The thick castle walls in her underground prison muffled her screams and cries for help. Without food or water or light, she slowly starved to death. Her passing from this world to the next was torturous and agonizing. Lady Margaret never did make a successful transition from life to death. Since her tortured passing, Lady Margaret has become known as the White Lady of Berry Pomeroy Castle. If you see her apparition, you should be very afraid. Her spirit's goal is to lead others to their graves.

The White Lady wanders the dungeons beneath St. Margaret's Tower, drifting up to the ramparts, calling out to anyone who will hear her. She begs the unsuspecting to join her in her eternal suffering. Those who have seen her report that hers is a horrifying specter. They experience thoughts of suicide and depression, mingled with terror.

Lady Margaret is not the only female ghost locked between life and death within the walls of Berry Pomeroy Castle. There is another spectral being, a malevolent spirit who lurks in the narrow passages and dank dungeons of this ancient Norman castle.

She is called the Blue Lady of Berry Pomeroy. If you should come face to face with her ghost, turn and run for your life, for she is even more malicious than the ghost of Lady Margaret. Do not make the mistake of listening to her, for she is not to be trusted.

Sightings of the Blue Lady date back to the 18th century. The whole castle is her haunt. She drifts from room to room, wearing a flowing blue cape and a similarly colored hood. In life, the Blue Lady was the daughter of a sadistic Norman lord and eventually gave birth to his child, a healthy boy. Sadly, the boy did not live for very

Two sisters are behind one of the hauntings at Berry Pomeroy Castle near Devon, England.

long. His tiny life was snuffed out when he was strangled in one of the upper rooms of the castle. Whether the shamed girl strangled him herself or whether he died at the hands of the sadistic baron is in dispute, but we do know that the Blue Lady lived out the rest of her life in misery, and died in regret.

The Blue Lady's face, according to those terrified witnesses who have seen her, reflects her sad, abused life. The Seymour family, who own the castle, know that her ghost is a portent of death: to see her is to see one's own mortality.

She only appears to those whose days are numbered. She particularly despises men, whom she tries to lure into unsafe areas of the castle where an "accidental death" is possible. Who can blame her? She has never forgiven her dangerous father.

Incredibly enough, there are even more paranormal occurrences at Berry Pomeroy Castle. They include strange orbs, shadowy figures, ice-cold winds, ectoplasm swirling at the tower base and strange sounds. Some of these sounds—disembodied screams and the thud of bodies hitting the ground—are associated with two Pomeroy brothers, who found themselves trapped in Berry Pomeroy Castle by a marauding force. Rather than surrender, they donned their full armor, mounted their horses and rode them at a full gallop to the ramparts where they plunged to their deaths on the cliffs below.

Berry Pomeroy Castle is one of those rare places where the line between the past and the present—and between the living and the dead—is blurred. Visit it by all means, but be prepared for anything.

Come Die with Me
TATTLETOWN, OHIO

Some earthbound spirits are malevolent in nature: they reach up from the grave to destroy those who have hurt or betrayed them in life. In this story, the ghost refused to rest until the loved one she left behind joined her in death. It is hard to feel anything but sympathy for her victim. If he was guilty of anything, it was only of trying to rebuild his life following the premature death of his wife.

If her behavior after she passed on is any indication, Mary Angle Henry must have been a difficult woman in life. As a young woman of marrying age, she caught the eye of James K. Henry, one of the most eligible bachelors in the village of Tattletown, Ohio. Unfortunately, James Henry made the fatal error of courting two women at once, and the hatred that ensued between them would prove his undoing.

Even though Mary Angle won the battle for James Henry's heart, it was a close race, and she continued to harbor an unnatural animosity for her one-time rival in love, Rachel Hodge. Following her marriage to James, Mary found it increasingly difficult to quell the jealousy that she felt for the only other girl James had been interested in. Mary mistrusted her husband and was loath to let him out of her sight.

James hoped that when Mary became pregnant with their first child she would become less insecure, but as the arrival date neared her behavior only worsened. Still, he was an optimistic man who believed that one day his young wife would become less suspicious. He never had a chance to find out. Mary's labor was long and difficult and, although she managed to deliver a healthy baby, she gave her life in the process. James buried her in the Tattletown graveyard and became a grieving widower.

Rachel Hodge bided her time but kept up a friendship with James that eventually developed into love. Three years after Mary died, James and Rachel exchanged marriage vows. James was thankful at being offered another chance at happiness. It was not to be. Shortly after he brought his new wife home, he made his weekly trek to put fresh flowers on Mary's grave. He was puzzled to see the outline of a horseshoe etched on her gravestone. A sense of foreboding descended on him. He didn't mention the strange phenomenon to Rachel, but he was troubled. Every night he prayed that his dead wife would not exact vengeance from the grave. He knew it was ridiculous to fear a dead person, but he had lived with Mary long enough to understand her powerful personality.

Less than a week after the horseshoe shape appeared on her gravestone, James K. Henry was kicked to death in the barn by the horse Mary had loved. He was buried beside his first wife. That was a long time ago, but the people who live near the Tattletown Cemetery claim that a strange light illuminates Mary's gravestone sometimes at night. The horseshoe becomes more visible with the passage of time, but the most eerie occurrences involve the shape of two women within its boundaries. They face each other aggressively and some say that the rivalry they initiated in life continues in death.

The Boiling Springs Hotel
BOILING SPRINGS, WEST VIRGINIA

When people make the mistake of confusing obsession for love, the results can be disastrous for all involved, as the following story so tragically illustrates.

At one time, the Boiling Springs Hotel in beautiful West Virginia was a popular resort for tourists. They calmed their restless minds by walking on the winding trails that surrounded the hotel or soothed their aching bodies in the healing natural mineral waters. It was a popular year-round destination with a loyal following of repeat guests.

Today it sits empty. The building has fallen into disrepair and nature has reclaimed much of the land surrounding it. But while the hotel sits empty, a lot of unusual activity takes place within its abandoned rooms. Years ago a terrible tragedy occurred at the Boiling Springs Hotel that resulted in the closing of its doors. Three guests died there under terrible circumstances. Their ethereal footsteps are still heard walking the deserted hallways and rooms, and their plaintive moans reverberate throughout the hotel.

Mr. Grayson and Mr. Miller were strangers when they arrived at the hotel for their vacations, but their mutual interest in the lovely Miss Pearson, another guest, quickly forced them into each other's company. The two suitors did not like each other from the start, but as they fought to gain Miss Pearson's attentions, the animosity between them increased. Miss Pearson did little to alleviate their stress. She encouraged one and then the other, never showing a preference for either one and adding to their mutual jealousy. Their pent-up emotions finally erupted in vicious fistfight on the front lawn of the hotel.

Boiling Springs Hotel is perched on the edge of a steep cliff overlooking a sweeping cultivated valley. Signs warned visitors to keep a safe distance, but Mr. Grayson and Mr. Miller were too embroiled in their battle to pay attention to their surroundings. The other hotel guests tried desperately to warn them of the drop that lay only inches away, but it was too late. Both men plunged to their deaths. Neither won the battle for the love of a woman.

Miss Pearson realized that she was at the root of the tragedy. If she had been more honest, they would not have died so unnecessarily. All along she had secretly harbored an attraction for Mr. Miller. Now she regretted terribly that she had never spoken up. The power she had enjoyed by encouraging both men was now equaled by the shame and guilt she felt at not admitting that she had already chosen one to be her fiancé.

Miss Pearson was unable to come to terms with what she had done. Early the next morning, she flung herself from the rocky precipice and died in the same spot as her suitors had.

The hotel proprietor was horrified at the scandal created by the misguided lovers. He did everything he could to quell the rumors that now surrounded his hotel, but the restless ghosts of Mr. Miller, Mr. Grayson and Miss Pearson refused to cooperate. Instead of passing over to the next world, they lingered at Boiling Springs. Of course none of the guests were comfortable sharing their rooms with the spirits of the dead, so they began to vacate the hotel en masse.

Within 12 months, the Boiling Springs Hotel closed its doors for the last time. Even the staff could not bear to sleep there. They complained of its dark ambiance and were unable to sleep because of the eerie sounds that filled the hotel at nightfall. As for the spirits of the three unhappy guests, they remain at the site of the hotel to this day, forever joined in their unhappy love triangle.

The Phantom Schooner
HARPSWELL HARBOR, MAINE

What flecks the outer gray beyond
The sundown's golden trail?
The white flash of a sea-bird's wing,
Or gleam of slanting sail?
Let young eyes watch from Neck and Point,
And sea-worn elders pray—
The ghost of what was once a ship
Is sailing up the bay!

— John Greenleaf,
The Dead Ship of Harpswell

At dusk, on misty, fog-shrouded evenings, the phantom ship *Sarah* cuts through the waters of the bay under full sail, visible only to those who will soon be visited by the Grim Reaper. Manned by the sailors who were murdered in cold blood on her maiden voyage nearly a century ago, the ill-fated schooner delivers her chilling message of death before she vanishes into the vapor as inexplicably and quickly as she appeared.

What lies between what men dream and what men realize? Often a woman, and in the case of George Leveret and Charles Jose, it was Sarah, the daughter of the owner of Soule Shipyard in Freeport, Maine. The two friends were young and their dreams for their futures were ambitious but realistic. In the early 1800s, traders could make a fortune plying goods up and down the Eastern Seaboard between North America and the West Indies, and that is just what the two young men planned to do.

George and Charles commissioned Soule Shipyard to build their vessel. While the schooner was under construction, both men fell in love with the shipbuilder's daughter, and their close bond quickly became a heated rivalry. Soon their partnership and their friendship lay in ruins—causalities of their battle for her attentions. Sarah showed interest in both the men, flaming their jealousy, but in the end she chose the calmer George to be her husband over the more hot-blooded Charles.

Rejected and hurt, Charles left Freeport determined to exact revenge upon his one-time friend. His love for Sarah had become an obsession, and he vowed to himself that George would pay a high price for stealing her heart.

Meanwhile, the ship was completed on schedule. George, seemingly lucky both in love and in business, proudly christened her *Sarah* after his fiancée. But from the day of her launch, *Sarah* seemed plagued by unusual problems. Sailors, usually plentiful in Freeport, proved difficult to hire, and many quit before *Sarah* left her homeport. Deck hands often have a sixth sense about doomed ships, and in the case of George Leveret's ship, their suspicions would be justified.

Finally a crew was found and *Sarah* set sail on her maiden voyage. George Leveret left Freeport bound for Portland Harbor, with the memory of his fiancée's parting kiss on his lips and visions of his success as a trader in his imagination. In Portland he filled *Sarah*'s hold with lumber and cod for his first trading trip south. It was here that the crew noticed an ominous black schooner docked nearby. She flew no flags and displayed no identification, and she made everyone but George very nervous.

The mystery ship stayed in Portland Harbor while *Sarah* prepared to set sail for her southern destination. If George Leveret had any concerns about her, he kept them to himself, instead concentrating on the long journey that lay ahead, and reassuring his unusually anxious crew. Finally the day arrived in November when *Sarah* tasted the salt air in her fully rigged sails. She sliced through the water like a knife through butter—an admirable example of the workmanship of the highly skilled boat-builders of Freeport's Soule Shipyard.

Now little more than a black spot on the horizon, the unidentified schooner sped to overtake *Sarah*. At her helm, Charles Jose, driven by revenge and blood lust, pushed his dark craft to her limits. He caught up with his enemy's ship and, like high-seas pirates, he and his men boarded the trading ship and began their evil work. Only when *Sarah*'s decks were stained crimson by the blood of her crew and the ship had been ransacked did Charles Jose order the killing to stop. One man still lived—George Leveret.

Charles Jose ordered George Leveret bound to the main mast by heavy rope. Then he set her sails and fastened her helm on a course to the open ocean. He and his men abandoned the dead ship, and George Leveret, barely conscious and his men dead at his feet, surrendered to fate. But while the situation seemed hopeless, he felt certain that his life would somehow be spared and that he would see his fiancée again.

What happened next has become legend in Maine. In front of George's disbelieving eyes, his slaughtered crew rose up, one after the other, and manned their stations. *Sarah* tacked and headed toward home. At Pott's Point, people on land watched incredulously as a beleaguered *Sarah* ploughed through the water, parallel to the shore, ignoring the laws of the wind and tide, until she came to a full stop. No sails were lowered, no anchor thrown to the ocean floor—*Sarah* hovered in a twilight zone, while her crew of dead men lowered an unconscious George Leveret into a skiff and rowed him to shore. They deposited him on a protected rock just above the water line.

The loyal crew from the nether-side then climbed into the little boat and disappeared into a heavy and sudden fog. It lifted as suddenly as it had descended, and when the air was clear, there was no sign of the battered *Sarah* or her ghostly crew.

When George Leveret was rescued, he was near death. His logbook lay safely beneath his body and from his lips he whispered a tale of murder and grace. George opted never to take to sea again. Jose disappeared without a trace, never to be seen again.

Sarah and her loyal crew of dead sailors did return, somehow bound to revisit Maine's coastline for years after their demise. Sightings were always followed by a death. Those who spotted the damaged schooner reacted in terror at the realization of their own mortality. It has been over 100 years since *Sarah*'s last sail-by, but the Soule Shipyard, a designated heritage building, is now in danger of being demolished. Perhaps if the people of Maine don't find a new home for this historical shipyard, *Sarah* and her doomed crew will return for a final farewell to their home port.

Lowther Castle
CUMBRIA, ENGLAND

Like a fair sister of the sky,
Unruffled doth the blue lake lie,
The mountains looking on.
　　　—William Wordsworth,
　　　　September 1819

When William Wordsworth penned these lines about the Lake District, he was thinking about his own childhood. He was raised in Cumbria, and he spent many happy days exploring the surrounding countryside. But for tourists who flock to the village of Cockermouth in northern England to visit the birthplace and childhood home of the brilliant poet, his upbringing is rarely as idealistic as they might imagine. Once they are able to unravel his life, many are surprised to discover that

Wordsworth's youth is forever linked to one of history's most despised men, Sir James Lowther. Sir James employed Wordsworth's father for many years. When the elder Wordsworth died prematurely, he left his children under the financial care of Sir James, a man described by biographer William Carlyle as "truly a madman, though too rich to be confined."

What follows is Sir James' story. While reading it, one cannot help but to ask oneself how good and evil could have lived side by side for so long.

Villagers and tradesmen traveling down the road that skirted Lowther Castle were the first to notice the putrid scent that seemed to be coming from the castle grounds. The rumors appeared to be true. Sir James had not buried the girl; instead, he had kept her corpse by his side. With each passing day, the stench of decaying flesh grew worse until even the air outside the castle was contaminated with the reek of death. Sir James Lowther seemed not to notice and nobody dared to bring it to his attention.

The dead girl lay in his bed, her vacant eyes fixed on another world. Her hands were folded over her sunken chest, and after so much time she had passed through the state of rigor mortis. Beneath her wasting form, the sheets were damp and stained yellow by bodily fluids that had leaked slowly out of her. In the beginning, Sir James used to dress her in clean clothes every morning and in the evenings he would prop her lifeless body up at the dinner table. His servants served her quickly then rushed from the dining room to spill the contents of their stomachs before returning to clear the table.

The dead girl's captor made light conversation with her as she sat with hollow eyes under his adoring gaze. He didn't seem to notice that she never replied. Finally the day came when even he could no longer inhale her scent or lift her body without pieces of it disintegrating in his hands. He took her from his bed and placed her in a glass coffin for all to see, even though no one, except himself, visited her. He didn't understand this. Why had her friends abandoned her?

Sir James Lowther had always been an obsessive man. Cruelly ambitious in both business and politics, he ruled his serfdom with an iron fist, never acknowledging the hatred and fear in the eyes of the people who depended on him for everything.

In 1784, he inherited Lowther Castle, an ominous fortress perched in the hills of England's Lake District, where pastoral meadows border clear lakes and rolling mountains. Soon after claiming his family seat, he entered into an arranged marriage that would further his aspirations but leave him in a loveless union. Even a man as cruel as Sir James Lowther craved happiness, and it was not long until he became romantically involved with a farmer's daughter. Sir Lowther's love quickly became his obsession, and her sudden passing—the result of a brief illness—proved his own downfall.

It is not likely that the girl he chose to shower his twisted attentions upon returned his feelings, or that she had any choice in the matter. More probable is that her own death was a result of finding herself the possession of a man possessed. Even though death offered an escape for her spirit, her body remained his for months following her passing. There was nothing her family could do. They were helpless in the face of his power.

And so the dead girl lay in a glass coffin until Sir James could not longer bear witness to the unrelenting passage of time. In the end he had little choice but to agree to her burial. She was interred in Paddington Cemetery in London, far from her home and her family. A company of Cumberland militia stood guard over her tomb.

Sir James Lowther returned to Lowther Castle a broken man. He slid into a dark depression and soon the little that remained of his sanity disappeared into a black hole dominated by his own chaotic thoughts of suicide and loss. As his mind broke down, so did his castle and the lands surrounding it. When Sir James Lowther died in 1802, the people of the Lake District rejoiced, but their relief was premature. Sir James was dead, but he was not gone. The first time his ghost made its presence known was as his coffin was lowered into the earth. It began to sway uncontrollably, and the graveyard workers dropped it. On the first full moon following his death, his frenzied ghost appeared on the grounds of Lowther Castle. After that, he returned every month, striking terror into the hearts of the people who ran into him.

Centuries later, a full moon above the town of Cockermouth and Lowther Castle is still an invitation for "Wicked Jimmy's" appearance in the parklands surrounding the castle. He usually appears sitting high in his carriage, whipping his spectral horses into a mad gallop that is without meaning or direction.

When the moon is full, the bitter spirit of Sir James Lowther steers his undead horses around the grounds of Lowther Castle.

Sir James was not a nice person in life. As Wordsworth's financial guardian, he was stingy and difficult to deal with. Nevertheless, Wordsworth went on to great things.

While the spirits of the people Lowther hurt in life have made the transition to the other side with ease, Sir Jimmy's ghost remains confused and lost. Today, it takes a brave person to wander the grounds of Lowther Castle on nights when the moon is full. Even those who are prepared for the ghostly visitor recoil in fear at the sight of him.

The End